T0167316

EXTREME
Love
MAY CAUSE
Death

Written by
JEFF O'DONNELL

in association with
DAUGHTER LURA SANCHEZ

Order this book online at www.trafford.com
or email orders@trafford.com

Most Trafford titles are also available at major online book retailers.

Print information available on the last page.

ISBN: 978-1-4907-8892-0 (sc)
ISBN: 978-1-4907-8891-3 (e)

Trafford rev. 05/10/2018

www.trafford.com
North America & international
toll-free: 1 888 232 4444 (USA & Canada)
fax: 812 355 4082

ABOUT THE AUTHOR

I GOT STARTED IN writing a few years back. My wife had A.L.S. and was bed ridden, I was her main care giver and was use to being very busy all day and night,when she died I was in a empty house and felt I should be doing something, there is where the book writing took hold. When I wrote I was not alone I had characters coming in and out of my head and I knew them all,that writing helped me from loneliness and depression. Now after years without writing I missed the people I would create,so I wrote this book. "Extreme Love May Cause Death." I truly hope you will enjoy this story.

THE QUIET WAS SHATTERED by "Bob! How many cards?" I'm staring at two kings, a pair of threes and a useless six of diamonds.

I quickly say, "One", while at the same time flipping my discard into the center of the table. The pot is already a good one, even before the draw; maybe close to $300. As the cards are dealt around the table I check out my chips neatly stacked in front of me. I figure I'm about a hundred bucks ahead and that is a real reversal from my usual luck at our weekly card game, held in the lounge of the Tennis & Yacht Club.

The dealer asks, "How many?" Most of the players take two or three cards. As the dealer throws the draw cards out, my single card sticks under my stack of chips. I take it by two fingers, slowly slide it out, anxious to see what I'd received. As I pull it towards me and turn up the top edge there it is, a beautiful king. I show no emotion and I just wait for the betting to begin. It starts off at the other end of the table. Mike opens with $10, then Hank sees his $10 and raises him $10. It was up to me. Should I go with a large bet and take the chance they will fold or will they think I'm trying to steal the pot with a bluff? I am GO. "I see the $20 and raise $80." I push my chips in.

Of the two players that follow my bet I lose one of them.

Mike is out first. "No way," he says as he throws his cards in. I wait for Hank's decision, suddenly I feel a hand on my shoulder. I slowly turn my head looking up at the same time. The first thing that catches my eye is a badge on a uniform. I know it's not a fireman's badge.

The young police officer has a buzz cut and the looks, of what I would imagine a male model on the cover of Esquire magazine would have.

"Mr. Raymonds?" he asks,

"Yes, may I help you?"

His immediate response, "May I speak with you for a moment outside?"

"Sure." Not knowing the severity of his message, I say out loud "Push all my chips in if Hank calls me."

The young cop puts his hand on my shoulder, "I really need to talk with you, sir."

I can tell in his voice and expression that something is up. No sooner do we step outside he tells me I need to get right home, there has been an incident

"What do you mean by incident?" I raise my voice.

The cop says, "I'm sorry that's all they told me."

"Who told you?"

"My supervisor just told me to find you and send you home and that's all I know."

I turn and take a half step back into the room and tell the gang "I got to go, I'll be in touch."

Hank yells out "Is everything O.K.?" While Mike asks about my chips.

As I turn and head out I yell, "I'll be in touch." As I'm walking at a half jog pace towards the parking lot my mind is going 100 times faster than my feet. What could have happened? My house was only a few miles away, but on this day, it seemed to be taking me forever

When I turn the corner onto my street it's quite apparent that something disastrous had taken place. There are two police cars, one ambulance, a fire truck and countless unmarked cars. I couldn't even get in my own driveway. There is yellow crime tape from my neighbor's fence on my right to my other neighbor's tree on my left. As I try to make it inside my house I am stopped by a uniformed cop who looks like he is working well past his retirement age and well past his original uniform size. As I lift the crime tape to crawl underneath he informs me, "Son, you'll have to stay back."

I don't know what irritates me more, being told to get back or being called son. I back off from the crime tape, I stand and yell, "God damn it! This is my house! Where is my wife? Where is Maria my housekeeper!?"

"Oh, I'm very sorry but I'll need to see some I.D. before I can let you enter the crime scene area." the fat cops notifies me.

"What the fuck are you telling me? What kind of crime scene are you talking about?" I snap back. With that sudden outburst, it gets the attention of a plain clothes detective who comes over.

He lifts the tape up. "Please come with me and I will try and explain what we know so far." As we approach the front door of my house we stop and the detective offers me his card and introduces himself as Detective Hamilton. A very slim, tall man with a slick back pompadour.

"We were called by Maria your house keeper. She is fine the paramedics took her to the hospital for precaution. She is very upset and they had a hard time calming her down. They thought it was best, I guess. Apparently she told 911 that your wife was unresponsive and locked inside one of your rooms. The fire department was called and an emergency response unit was sent, but I'm very sorry to tell you that she was deceased when we arrived."

"Deceased! What are you talking about? How? I want to see her!" As I head towards my front door I'm pulled back with a slight tug on my shoulder.

Det. Hamilton tries to calm me. "Mr. Raymonds. I can't let you in just yet. I'm sure you understand there's quite a group in there collecting evidence."

"Why are you collecting evidence? Are you telling me this was not a death by natural causes?"

"No, I'm not telling you anything of the sort. I'm telling you, we are looking for the cause of your wife's death. We don't assume anything. We go on hard evidence and that's what we are looking for now. I want to let you know I'm not the one who will be handling this case. I am due to testify in court. Two detectives have already been assigned. Believe me, these guys are sharp. So, please stay outside and let us do our job and we will give you the ok to go in when we're done."

With that he goes inside my house. I pace outside waiting. I hear voices and see two officers lifting the yellow tape for a vehicle to drive under. As it pulls directly in front of the house I read, Coroner Office, Santa Pauline County" on the door.

Two men in dark blue coveralls with the words Coroner Department stenciled on the back get out of the van. They walk to the back of the vehicle and systematically pull out a gurney. As the two of them wheel by me without the slightest recognition of my presence, I feel sick to my stomach. I have mixed emotions. I want to see her face. After all, maybe it wasn't Viv, but then again, I don't want to see her like that. I feel as I'm going to throw up. I make my way back to my car.

Before I can open the driver's door, my neighbors come at me from all sides, kids on bikes, neighbors walking their dogs and of course, news reporters. They all surround me, everyone one of them asking questions at the same time. I can't make out what they are saying, it all blends into one big blur.

I stand at my driver's door, set both of my hands on the roof of the car and tell everyone in ear shot, "I don't have any information on anything and when I know something I'll let you all know. I would appreciate if everyone would just give me some privacy. Thank you."

I slide into the driver's seat and quickly search for the handle to set my seat back into the reclining position. I can see a group of neighbors and strangers gathering. A news crew making their way from their van. I guess in the back of their minds they know someone was dead in that house and possibly they could be looking at a cold-blooded murderer, cell phones come out and up. News crews weren't going to be the only ones with footage. Either way I'm relieved to be alone in my car. A wave of exhaustion comes over me, One minute I'm excited about my potential winning hand in a poker game the next minute I'm told my wife is dead. I close my eyes; my eyelids feel like they are made from lead. I can feel the warmth of the sun streaming through the windshield and it's all I need to fall into thoughts of Viv and me in the early days of our courtship and marriage.

My thoughts go deeper and to the later years when not only were we losing our marriage we were losing our love and respect for each other. There were times she hurt me so deeply I could have killed her. In fact- I was having recurring dreams about how I could do away with her. I hear a tap, tap, tap, and open my eyes to see a uniformed cop tapping on my window with his night stick.

"Mr. Raymonds, you had me worried there for a minute, you feel ok?"

"Yes I am fine. Can I go in now?"

"Yes, they told me to come and let you know you can go right in. Your wife has been taken away I just wanted you to know that."

I say, "Thanks." I get out of the car and head for my front door and entry way.

As I walk up the front porch steps, all four of them. Everything looks normal and nothing seem to be amiss. That is until I enter the actual house itself.

The first thing I do is step over the wood that used to be part of a door frame to the recreation room or better known as simply the Rec. Room. As I walk by what I assumed was the crime scene I see a couple of guys still picking up items and dusting for fingerprints.

One of them looks over at me and puts his hand up to stop me. "Mr. Raymonds we will be concluding in a few moments. Please stay back." With that his hand goes back down and continues whatever he is doing. I can't stand to look at the carnage that is left behind. Dejected and numb I slowly walk upstairs to my bedroom. Viv and I had not shared the same bedroom for quite a while. Things had turned sour over the past couple of years, but I still loved her.

I take my shoes off and lay down. Here I was in what should be the prime of my life and it was slowly spiraling down and out of control. My first and only marriage was in shambles; my law career was on life support and now this. My wife killed herself or maybe had a heart attack? Did she forget how many drinks she had and mix in some of her pills? Did the detectives know I was a criminal lawyer? Everyone knows when a spouse dies, the surviving one is the prime suspect. I bet the cops knew more about this death than they let on….

I see myself standing off to one side in an unfamiliar room. I watch as my wife begins slumping ever so slowly to the floor. I watch as her expression changes from bewilderment to astonishment to horror. She couldn't grasp that her husband is following through. I feel delighted as she begins to contort in pain. I try to take it all in and save it in my mind. This is so enjoyable, I replay and relive the grandeur of my accomplishment. I feel so...

The sound of the bedroom curtains being pulled open make me realize I had fallen asleep on top of the covers with my clothes on.

I look in the direction of the very familiar ritual being performed by my housekeeper, Maria. Maria Sanchez looks older than her 41 years. Her eyes are sad and beat down from what I can only assume is years of hard manual work from a young age. She rarely talks about her marriage, from what I know they live separate lives. He lives down south for work and to be closer to his family. She has a sister who lives about 2 hours away she visits about twice a year and was "never blessed with children", her words. She takes pride in her work, her church and her cooking abilities. When I look at her today, I can see her eyes are red and swollen from crying

"Oh, Mr. Ray'" a name she has called me since I hired her right after my marriage to Viv. "I am so sorry about Miss Viv. I know you went upstairs last night and I just let you be. I just went to my room and tried to sleep, you know how I worry about you Mr. Ray."

I jump out of bed and give her a hug. "Worry about me, Maria?! Are you ok? The police told me you were taken to the hospital. I was going to go over there or call but I must have..."

She interrupts before I can even finish. "Mr. Ray I am ok, please don't worry about me. I was going to let you sleep but there are two policemen downstairs. They have many questions and they say for you to come now. They say they want to talk with you."

"They say? They say?" I answer in a somewhat irritated tone. "Fine, but they can wait until I shower. Are you sure you're alright Maria? Why don't you take some time off? Get away for a while."

"Oh no, Mr. Ray. I could not leave you at this time. You need someone to look after you, now that Mrs. Ray... "She daps her eyes every so gently with the towel she always keeps tucked in the waist band of her uniform.

"Are you absolutely sure Maria?" I'm conflicted on what I think she should do. I know the news crew and the on lookers will be back, but I think in the past 9 years she only took off 5 days. And that was because Viv and I made her.

"Mr. Ray, I will tell them you be down after you shower and get dressed."

"That's right Maria. And you tell them if they don't like that, they can come back later."

"I go now and tell them what you say." When Maria leaves the room I head for the shower. My neck and back are in knots from tension so the water hitting my face feels peaceful and relaxing. I think to hell with the police they can wait for as long as it takes me to get ready. I'm sure Maria will get them coffee and danish.

As I reach the bottom of the staircase I'm greeted by two very young and well-groomed detectives. They could have been twins as far as I was concerned. Both are dressed in the same shade blue suit; same color ties, the only difference is one solid color while the other has a slight design. Looking at them further, I notice both have their hair cut in military style and to top it off, they are holding their coffee cup and saucer in the same hand.

"I sure hope you guys have name tags." Before they have a chance to respond, "Do you call each other the morning to see what the other is wearing?" I extend my hand in greeting. "Anyone ever tell you, look like twins?"

The one with the solid tie answers first. "Oh yeah, we get that, plus other not so flattering comments all the time. I am Detective Nick Andrews and this is my partner Detective Ryan White."

"So, tell me. Did you boys come this early to tell me you have information on my wife's death?"

"Mr. Raymonds, I'm sorry to tell you we don't have a definitive answer on that quite yet. I can tell you that nothing has been ruled out."

"What do you mean by that?"

"Well it could be natural causes, suicide, or even homicide. Do you understand what I mean by nothing can be ruled out, now?" Det. White's retort seems harsher than necessary.

"Well tell me this, detective? When are we going to get the results? It would help put my mind to rest. I hate the thought of her killing herself."

"You are assuming it was a suicide Mr. Raymonds." I think to myself that Det. White's people skills need work.

Det. Andrews with the design tie asks, "Did your wife try to harm herself in the past?"

As a criminal attorney I should be prepared for THAT question to be asked, but it catches me off guard. The detectives take notice and give each other a look.

"I was told she was in a locked room that the fire department had to break into. You can see for yourselves." I point in the direction of the Rec. Room

"Yes, but we still have questions we need to ask. Or we wouldn't be doing our jobs." Det. Andrews smiles a bit, maybe in an effort to soften me up.

"Well boys, I would love to answer your questions but I have a doctor's appointment that I can't miss. And since I really didn't know you guys were coming." I stand up in an effort to move them along. "If you give me your card I will set up an appointment to talk with you."

They stand up at the exact same time and both hand me their cards. "Oh, and if you have trouble telling us apart. I like to have a design and Det. White prefers a solid color."

"You must be the rebellious one. Like I say I'll give you a call." And with that I walk them to the front door. They both politely nod their heads."

"Just one question before we go Mr. Raymonds. Were you and your wife having any marital problems?" Det. White ask.

"Doesn't every married couple have some problems? I hold their card up, "I will be in touch." I shut the door before they can ask anything else.

No sooner I turn around my heart skips a beat. Standing behind me is Maria. She apologizes seeing me almost jump out of my skin, "Oh, I so sorry I scare you Mr. Ray."

"No, it's not your fault, I'm just a little jumpy."

"Si, I understand, that's how I was when Mrs. Ray didn't answer when I banged on the door. When I went outside and saw her laying on a couch and knocked real hard on glass door windows. She still didn't move. I knew then something was bad with her. I ran to tell man on phone I must call 911 number."

"What man?

"She got a phone call and the man said he had to speak to her right now. He said it was extremely important. I try to tell him that Mrs. Raymonds does not like to be disturbed. He yell at me saying get her ass on the phone now or believe me there will be hell to pay. He ask if I comprende. He scared me and I say I try to get her. But when I see her like that, I run to phone but he's not on it. I call 911 and the operator tries to give me instrucciones, but I tell her Mrs. Ray in a locked room. No key."

"You did wonderful Maria there was nothing more you could have done."

"Thank you Mr. Ray, that makes me feel better. I blame myself for knocking on door, I never do that before, and I know she doesn't like it. Maybe, I upset her very much and her heart stops?"

"No Maria. You didn't cause her any harm whatsoever."

"I sure hope you are right Mr. Ray."

I look over Maria's shoulder and can't help but see one of the double doors to the Rec. Room leaning against the wall just a few short feet from the front door entry way. By the looks of the surrounding area of the door, it must have been no easy task to access to the room, there are splinters of wood scattered from one end of the house to the other. The hinges are still in the door jam, the bolt lock still in the locked position, but that isn't surprising. Viv would bring her cocktail and the previous day's mail and lock herself away, it was her routine and Maria knew not to disturb her. I step over the splinters of wood and look in. It was the last place my wife was alive.

"Mr. Ray I will clean up this up right away. I can't believe I don't do it already."

My eyes scan the room, I remember Viv next to the French doors measuring for the curtains, and she was looking at me with a big smile," how's it going on your end?"

"Fine, I'm almost finished lighting the aquarium. It's going to look even better than I imagined."

We both had a hand in designing and furnishing the room and we both agreed it was awesome. It had two large flat screen TV's at each and of the room, a vintage pinball machine, two eight-foot leather couches with matching reclining chairs, but what I thought was the "coup de grace" that set the room apart from all others was the aquarium. It was set just left of the French doors that opened to the outdoor patio, the fish tank was just shy of 6 feet long and 2 feet wide. It really set off the room with its bright colors of artificial coral. You couldn't help but be mesmerized with the gentle bubbles and the fish gliding in and out among the tiny ancient Greek columns from a civilization vanished from time. It must be easy being a fish, no job, no taxes, and no sadness.

I hear swishing and turn quickly to see Maria straddling the broken shards of wood with a broom and dust pan. I look at my wrist watch I need to get my ass moving. At $325 an hour

I didn't want to be late even a minute. And I need to see the Doc more today than ever. I take a step past Maria and head upstairs to get a sports coat.

I go to my walk-in closet. Half of it used to belong to Viv, but when we had our split she went downstairs and took over the guest room as her own living space.

I hear a familiar voice coming from the bottom of the stairs. "Mr. Ray you better be going, do you see what time it is?"

I slide the coats along the stainless-steel rod. I just want something easy, something casual. I could quickly eliminate most of them due to my weight gain, or as Viv said were out of date or out of style or both in my case. One caught my eye that would work just fine. As I pull the hanger towards me I notice a small stain on one of the sleeves. I look closer to see what it is. I instinctively rub my thumb across it and it just crumbles like some sort of powder or dry paste. What the hell is this? I rub my thumb across it and it crumbles. When was the last time I wore this?

As I make my way down the stairs I yell out "Maria!"

She scurries from the Rec. Room, "yes what do you need Mr. Ray?"

"I was just wondering what day you go to the cleaners."

"I usually go on Thursday, but if you need me to go sooner I will."

"No, that won't be necessary just take this when you go." I hand her the stained sport coat.

I head out the door wearing a dress shirt with no coat. I turn in the direction of my driveway, not seeing my car in its usual place I momentarily panic. Then I remember my car being parked on the street. As I walk toward my car I rip apart the yellow crime tape left behind, somewhat pissed they didn't take it all down when they were finished. I feel myself instantly in a bad mood, pleading with God or Karma that I don't to run into any neighbors. I don't feel like answering any questions, especially since I don't have answers. Out of the corner of my eye I can see my next-door neighbor heading my way. God or Karma must not be listening because walking towards me is Larry Hamilton, a real pain in the ass. I get in the car as quickly as I can and give the impression I don't see or hear him call out my name.

It takes me no time to get to the doctor's office; after all living in a small town has its advantages, everything is a short distance from each other. I had started seeing Dr. Ratcliff about a year ago. It was the time Viv and I were starting to have a strain with our marriage. We had got to the point we didn't sleep in the same room, but it didn't stop her from having gentlemen callers over when I was at the office or in court. The deal we had was that she could do whatever she wanted when I was out of the house, but if I called saying I was on my way home she had to clear them out. It only took a few weeks of this arrangement and I started to dislike her, what am I saying, I despised her. That's when the dreams began.

I look at my watch as I pull my Cadillac into the handicapped parking space. I was right on the button for my appointment. I open the car door and step one foot out when I realize why I have the handicap sticker dangling from my rearview mirror. My back suddenly locks up and goes into spasms. I hold onto the top of the car door and try to stand up straight, I hold my breath and hope the spasm will go away in a few moments.

This whole back thing happened a few of years ago when a VERY disgruntled witness took exception to my cross examination As I was walking back to the defense table he jumped down from the witness stand grabbed the chair the court reporter had just been sitting in and smashed it into my back and ribcage. I was only seconds before two maybe three bailiffs had him subdued and in cuffs. I just laid on the floor, hearing the judge yell, "clear the court room." From that point I don't remember a thing until I was in the emergency room at our local hospital. For some unknown reason, maybe it was the morphine drip I was on; I thought I now know what Floyd Patterson felt like when Sonny Listen hit him

For me it took close to a year of physical therapy and a stab at acupuncture (get it?) But I guess what worked the best were the painkillers and strong muscle relaxers. I thought for a long time about that outburst and rage from a witness I cross-examined. What had I done this time that I hadn't done a hundred times before? Viv and I were together back then and when she came to see me in the hospital I asked her flat out,

"Did you see any reason why the witness went berserk on me?"

Viv said, "Only that you came across as an arrogant know-it-all prick and made him look like a stammering fool on the stand. I think the last straw for him was when you gave him a shrug and turned your back on him as you said, "No further questions your honor".

"No, I don't want you holding back, tell me what you really think?"

"Bob, when you first started as a defense lawyer you had principles and class, you played by the rules, you were respected, but after you became a household name your ego grew as much as your bank account and waist line."

"Don't you mean our bank account?" I replied.

"No, I mean your bank account. You're the one who went out and spent $75,000 on a car, $35,000 for a watch, maybe $2,000 for a suit and $500 for shoes."

"Hey, I want you to know the shoes were on sale, one third off."

"Very funny, but you're not the same man you used to be, you should consider counseling." Now you see where Dr. Radcliff comes in.

I now have done enough stretching along the side of my car that I can try to walk into the lobby of the medical building. The building is a five-story job that held the offices of doctors that worked on those with physical or mental issues. My doctor is located on the 4th floor so there would be no using the stairs for me. The elevator is quiet and smooth. The doors open as silent as a Venus Fly Trap. I am standing directly in front of Dr. Ratcliff's office. As I walk right in I see the waiting room is empty and his office door wide open. This was a sign for scheduled patients to come right in. He must have heard the door open or my footsteps, because he was in his doorway before I reach it.

"Please come in Bob". He pushes the door wider and steps back to let me through. I know the routine so I assume my position at the end of the couch. (I sit) I don't know if anyone lies down anymore? I look over at the Doc and he already has his notepad in hand and is in his swivel chair. He wears pretty much the same thing whenever I see him; dark slacks, a Cosby sweater (no matter the season) and the professor sport coat including the patches on the elbows. Now throw in his well-trimmed white beard and outdated reading glasses and you have the prototype psychiatrist.

I sit in silence waiting for the good doctor to say something about Viv's death. The game of silence is both awkward and as they say, deafening. I feel the doctor has the upper hand when he sets down his pad and pen, and leans back in his chair with his hands clasped behind his head. Surprisingly he speaks first. "Bob, are you sure you want to spend your money like this? I mean you've got 50 minutes and you can just sit there if you want, but I personally don't think that's going to help you much?"

It was then I realize he doesn't know a thing about Viv's death. "Did you see this morning's paper?" I assumed the death would be front-page news, After all, I was the famous defense lawyer Robert Raymond's. "Doc...Viv died yesterday."

"Oh no! Bob, I'm sorry. What happened?"

"I don't know, the police aren't telling me much. She was brought to the coroner's office yesterday"

"What are you thinking Bob? You are not only the husband but a criminal lawyer. You must have several thoughts and feelings about Viv's passing."

"I don't know, Doc! I'm headed over there after this appointment. It's the shits not knowing what happened to her."

He hesitates before he asks, "Bob, do you think you had anything to do with it? We have discussed the recurring dreams of killing her."

"Jesus H Doc! There are a couple of things that need to be investigated before I should consider myself prime suspect. I was at the yacht club from mid-morning until they came and gave me the news. I don't know exact time of death but that's a pretty strong alibi. And the cause would be very important don't you think? I mean there is the possibility of suicide."

"Suicide? Why would you say that?" he asks.

I begin talking louder out of frustration, "I'll tell you why, the fire department had to be called in to knock down the door, she was in a locked room that was locked from the inside, you know the kind you need to lock and unlock by hand. So, I'm thinking it's suicide or accident or some kind or natural causes."

"Ok Bob. I understand this is all very overwhelming. The combination of those dreams and the wishful thinking talk. Do you feel you are in emotional turmoil?"

"To tell you the truth, I feel..." I try to choose the right words. It's not nearly as satisfying as I thought. In fact, I'm glad I didn't kill her, if that turns out to be the case"

"Are know you are joking Bob, but I have to ask. Are you certain you had nothing to do with it? There was a lot of rage and anger towards Vivian."

"I'm fairly certain, unless I sleep walk and know of a way of getting into a looked room."

I for once look at my watch and say what he usually says every week. "Well it looks like our time is up." I get up quick, feeling a sharp pain in my lower back, I walk over to the Doctor, extend my hand, but he grabs me by the wrist, pulls me close and gives me a half hug,

"I'm truly sorry for your loss. You may have had your problems but she was your wife." I felt somewhat uncomfortable with his hug and his words. "Thanks Doc, I got

to run I need to talk with the police. I will see you next week."
I am, out the door and in the parking lot in a moment's time. I
quickly hop in the car the best I could with my back as tight as
it is. I carefully lean over to the passenger side and pop open
the glove compartment looking for some pain pills, I usually
keep a few for times like this. I move all the unnecessary
paperwork, pens, pencils, disposable cameras, and God knows
what else but the search is a success. I found 3 pills in an
unmarked prescription container, but I know what they are.
Hot sellers in the black market today, oxycodone. I take one
out and swallow it whole without water. I think about taking
another but decide against it. I fasten my seatbelt, adjusted my
rearview mirror which I do unconsciously every time I get into
the car and look at my reflection. I see no sorrow or grief in
my face, but I feel something in the pit of my gut. I know it's
not the pill I took dry. It's something else. Am I in shock? I
the Doc right and I'm in emotional turmoil or denial? After
all I felt no emotions, sadness, happiness, or anger. I have no
feelings. I'm just numb and is that a good sign or bad?

I look behind me, put the car in reverse and head out of the
half-filled parking lot. Time to ask and answer some questions
at the police department.

The drive is short and I pull into the underground garage
where the police share the building and parking lot with the
city offices. I find a handicap spot right next to the elevators.
When I get out of my car I expect to feel a sharp pain, but
nothing. The pill is working. I get in the elevator but have
no idea what floor I am looking for, lucky for me they have a
complete list with building numbers, framed behind scratched
plexy glass by the elevators. It shows everything from where to
pay parking tickets, get building permits, licenses for marriage
and dogs; the whole gamut of needs and services.

I check the directory and find what I think would be my
category; Homicide & Investigations 2nd floor room 17. I step
in the elevator which seemed to be waiting for my arrival, hit

the button the door closes and I feel the sudden lurch of the elevator making its ascension. I think boy what a difference between this elevator and the one at my doctor's office. The doors open slowly like they had been denied oil or WD-40 for many years. I look up and I'm staring at "2nd floor" on the wall in very large letters.

Below the 2nd floor sign are directions for the offices with faded green arrows pointing odd numbers to the right, even to the left. With a quick turn to the right I head to room 17. I walk right in and see a counter with three computers on top and two police officers one male, one female both in full uniform looking at the monitors with a blank stares. I immediately think of the movies "Invasion of the Body Snatchers" and "The Stepford Wives." I'm the only one in the room so I walk right up to the counter and chose the young female who seems friendlier. She is enthralled with what she is viewing on the screen but eventually breaks away and looks at me. For a second her eyes are blank as though she has no soul and I think to myself I should have picked the male officer, but then just as fast she smiles and says, "May I help you?" When she does that she reminds me of Angie Dickinson from the classic 70's show "Police Woman".

"I would like to speak with someone regarding my wife's death."

In an almost sweet tone she asks, "Name of the Detectives handling the case?"

I fumble to search my pockets to find their card but have no luck.

Officer (Dickson) sees my feeble attempt, "Name of the decease?"

"Vivian Raymonds"

She quickly punches the keyboard and picks up the phone as she points and instructs me to take a seat along the wall. There is a row of chairs that must be from the late 50's or early 60's. They are the kind you would find in beauty shops or barber shops back in day. With rounded chromed metal arms and backing. The seats are covered in light green Naugahyde.

"I have to ask, where did you get these chairs?"

"Oh, aren't those great! One of our retired officers donated them. His family owned a large beauty shop and barber shop and when they sold the business they got to keep all the furniture and equipment. The new owners thought everything in the shop was outdated and obsolete."

"Well, that was very generous on his part. These chairs are classic and much sought after. They are like old Coke machines you can almost name your own price." I was just kidding but I don't think she knew it.

"I agree." You have a seat and Det. White or Det. Andrews will be right with you."

"Thanks." I look around for some magazines, but nothing. For being 70 years old chairs they are pretty comfortable as long as you didn't try to sit in them during the summer wearing shorts, as I recalled. I look at my watch, it's almost 3:30. Not knowing how long it will take, I lean my head back against the wall and close my eyes. The pain pills were relaxing more than just my back muscles. I start to feel very drowsy. The sounds of the office seem almost soothing; my ears could hear conversations, phones ringing, fax machines spitting out papers; almost like hearing ocean waves splashing against the shore. I find it hypnotic. I couldn't help but start thinking about why I was here and how it came to be.

Viv and I started out so good. It was true love, but then the cheating, lying and the escalating arguments. When the neighbors started calling the police we knew it was time to do something about our living arrangements. I must admit the end of our relationship was a sad one, but the beginning was so romantic and exuberant. I looked forward to each day. I remember when we met...

It was a victory celebration for a client, James 'Big Jim' Marshall a very confident and arrogant businessman. I didn't really care for the guy but he gave the firm a very large retainer which we couldn't pass up. This guy was so confident I would win his case he reserved the restaurant in a high priced plush hotel. He was more confident then I was but his faith in me turned out prophetic. Won the case which very much pleased the both of us.

When I entered the celebration party I was greeted with a round of applause. I waved my arms like Dick Nixon not leaving out the "V" for victory with my fingers. Without slowing my stride I preceded directly to the bar. As I made my approach I passed people on my left and right some reaching out and patting me on my shoulders. I felt like a rock star. Most of the people at the party I didn't recognize, they seemed to be Mr. Marshall's friends and associates.

My client Mr. Marshall, waved me over to his location at the bar, it was apparent he had gotten an early start on the celebration with more than a few cocktails. He greeted me not with a handshake but a bear hug. It was at that moment that I saw her, a tall slender woman with the looks of a Cover Girl and the body of a swimsuit model, I was locked in on every move she made. Our eyes met for a moment, but I was literally shaken out of it when Mr. Marshall takes my shoulders. With a firm grasp and a spray of spittle he tells me, "kid, if you ever need anything you name it." Without missing a beat he reaches for the glass sitting on the bar, grabs it without looking and chugs it.

I looked him in the eye," I have one immediate request, something you can do for me."

"You name it," his words slur a bit.

"Well I wouldn't mind it if you introduced me to," then nodding in her direction, "the tall beauty laughing with that older guy in the bow tie. Over there"

Mr. Marshall turns around and laughs." I don't blame you a bit. That's Vivian Lynch. She used to work for me at one of my distribution warehouses as a clerk or accountant, something like that, I don't remember exactly?" He raises his hand and flags one of the bartenders and gives the circling motion with his index finger, another round for his group. Then he leans into me," you know I had to let her go she was causing quite a disturbance on the dock. I mean guys were finding one reason after another to come into the office and talk with her. Talking about their checks, their overtime hours all bullshit stuff really. I felt kind of bad, she's a good kid. Just too damn good looking with a knockout body." His drink arrives and he stirs it with his finger ignoring the swizzle stick sticking out of the glass and downs it faster than last one.

"You know I gave her name out to some of my business partners thinking they could find something for her? I never heard back, so I don't know if she ever landed anything?" Then he gives me a hard slap on my shoulder, "hey let's get you guys hooked up."

He sets down his empty glass and takes me by the hand as though I was his child and leads me down to the end of the bar. He promptly and rudely squeezes between bowtie man and Vivian. "Miss Vivian Lynch may I introduce you to a very good friend of mine and one hell of a lawyer, Mr. Raymonds, Mr. Robert Raymonds."

She tries to look around and over Marshall to get a glance at me, what she sees is a man sporting a huge smile. She reaches over his shoulder extending her hand, I in turn grab her hand holding it firmly but not too tight as to cause her discomfort. I was instantly taken by her warmth and infectious smile; we continue to hold hands as we moved around our introducer and start to talk.

"So, the word is you got Big Jim off."

"Excuse me? I did nothing of the sort. I don't swing that way."

"Very funny, you know what I mean. That man is as phony as a $2 bill."

"Don't you mean $3 bill? You know there are such things as two-dollar bills."

"Very funny." She looks at a wrist watch. I'm nervous that she is going to make an excuse to leave.

"Well, tell me why do you call Mr. Marshall, Big Jim?"

"He told me to. That's what he likes to be called. He tells me he has a big bank account, a big personality and a big you know what."

"Thank YOU very much. That's a visual image I don't need." Vivian leaned into me as she reached for a napkin from the stack that was on the bar. She smelled comforting, like when your mom takes out a tray of freshly baked cookies from the oven. It was right then and there I didn't want the night to end. I wanted to know everything about her.

All of sudden my dreaming of days gone by was shattered; it was the subtle sound of a female voice. I open my eyes, "Mr. Raymonds, Detective White would like to speak with you." With that she opens a small swinging gate that blended in with the counter and motions for me to follow her. She leads me a short distance to a door that has a protruding sign above it stating Homicide Department and just like Vanna White revealing a letter shows me to a door. She gives me a parting view and heads back to her post, as I watch her walk away, I suddenly feel a twinge of guilt by doing so. Now it was time to walk in and see what information the police had and what they would tell me. With a bit of trepidation I open the door. The room is larger than I expected. There are four or five large cubicles, the one closest to the door has an opening facing the door. Getting up from his desk is one of the Detective Twins, which one I don't know.

"Nice to see you again Mr. Raymonds. Let's go to where we can talk. Can I get you a coffee or water?"

"No thanks I'm good but you can remind me if you're Andrews or White?"

"Oh, I'm sorry. I'm Detective Andrews. How are you doing today? How did the appointment go?"

"Fine. Do you have any information for me?" Standing there I feel like an uninvited relative during the holidays; very uncomfortable.

"Could you please follow me Mr. Raymonds?" He leads me into one of the generic cubicles and offers me a seat. My uncomfortable feeling goes up a notch like when you're in a public restroom and there is no door on the stall.

"Relax Mr. Raymonds you look so anxious."

"Well, I am. What did the cornor come up with?"

"That's why I brought you back here instead of me going up to the front counter. The coroner gave me his report and he said he has never seen anything like it in his career. I haven't been around as long as he has but this one is a real head-scratcher."

"Just what are you trying to tell me?"

"Well, I'll try and explain it. Unless you know how to read x-rays?"

I don't bother to answer that question. My attorney senses start to tingle.

"But that wouldn't help you much with the answers because no one here can figure out what we have."

"Well how about going real slow and tell me what you do know and forget about what you don't."

"Ok. We do know it's a puncture wound through the heart."

"So if I was a detective, which I'm not, I would assume she set the knife in such a position she could fall onto it using her own weight."

"I wish we could use that as one of our options for cause of death."

"And why has that possibility been ruled out? After all she was in a locked room it had to be a self-inflicted wound, what else could it be?"

"Your guess is as good as ours, we looked for a secret entrance from top to bottom in that room and there was nothing. Your wife was locked in that room, but here is the real puzzling part of her death, she had a hole through her heart, but there was no hole through her blouse or bra and the corner describes the wound from an unknown source."

"What does that mean?"

"Well it wasn't a knife, scissors, screwdriver, or even an ice pick. He is completely baffled He has sent out an email to other jurisdictions seeking advice to see if anyone else has come across such an injury. He also has a call out to FBI.

"I don't understand. If a weapon of ANY type was used, it would still be in the locked room or am I missing something?"

"No, you're not missing anything. We're asking ourselves the same questions you are asking right now. We have even contemplated her heart could have imploded but the tissue samples don't indicate that. As far as our medical examiner is concerned the skin and tissue showed a puncture like injury. If it was an imploded injury the tissue and skin would be pushing in an out-word fashion. He said he has never seen anything like this in his professional life. But he also said he's never seen human combustion."

"What you're telling me is you don't have any answers? Give me a call when you have some solid information otherwise I have things I need to prepare for," and with that I get up to leave not bothering to shake his hand

Before I completely walk out the door, Det. White steps into the room almost has if he is trying to block my exit.

"Mr. Raymonds? Now that we have answered your questions. We have a few of our own we would like to ask you."

"Of course. I have no problem answering your questions. Unfortunately, I have some arrangements I need to take care of. I will schedule a time to talk with you or your partner - But I really need to go."

Det. White very loudly says, "sooner rather than later Mr. Raymonds."

As I walk out through the waiting room Officer (Dickson) says, "Hope to see you again." She says it with such conviction, I don't think she realizes no one wants to be seen again at the Homicide Department.

I make my way back to my car and just sit in the driver seat not feeling up to driving in traffic or even leaving my parking space. I feel my shoulder's sag and my head drop. I'm not only physically exhausted but more mentally. I also wonder if my pain pills are much more effective with my body resistance so low.

I grab the side handle on the seat and get myself in the reclining position, I close my eyes, and I feel I haven't slept in days. I think back when I thought I had things under control. My business had been very prosperous, things were good with Viv. It was probably the happiest days of my life. I couldn't explain my relationship with Viv but there was a connection between us, we were always on the same wavelength. On one occasion I was craving Italian food and without telling her about my desire she recommended the best Italian restaurant in town. It went the same with music, if I wanted to hear classical while we went on a trip, she would grab the same C.D. I would have chosen. It seemed like at times she was clairvoyant.

The term soul mate in my estimation is an overused term, but I believe it fit perfectly for the two of us. Back in our early days of dating it seemed like I was always in a good mood, she made me happy and she made me feel I was accomplishing something positive when I went to court, she made me a better lawyer. After six months maybe less, there was no doubt I wanted to marry her.

I hear the sound of a car horn honking, I open my eyes and realize I'm in my car. "Jesus, I must have been out cold." I reach down pull the handle and get myself in the upright position. My head is still a little groggy but had to get on the road. I adjust the rear view mirror and see someone that look like they just woke up- imagine that?!

I am so tired and drained emotionally? The loss of Viv has hit me hard and the pills, alcohol and police inquest doesn't help

As I drive, I try not to dwell on the negatives of the recent past and try to enjoy the thoughts of happier days. How truly lucky I was that a beautiful 28-year-old would accept my proposal for marriage. It would be the first marriage for both of us. I at 40 never thought I would ever find "The One." Our plans were for a small wedding nothing extravagant, it would be immediate relatives and a few close friends. She stipulated one condition: No Big Jim!

"Come on Viv, without him, there would be no us," I joked.

She gave me "That Look" the one that told me I was not going to dissuade her into changing her mind. From that point the subject was dropped. In the back of my mind I always felt there was much more to the story than she let on, but I wasn't stupid enough to get on her bad side right before the wedding. The wedding was perfect; Viv was an absolute knock out, and when looking at her, again I thought how in the world did I land her? The day was over before we knew it and that was just fine with me, I wanted to get to the airport and fly off and start our honeymoon in the Romantic Paradise of Trinidad.

The honeymoon was fantastic. We did ALL the romantic things one does on their honeymoon; laying by the pool, laying on the beach and lying in bed. We were like two teenage lovebirds.

When we got back to the States it was balls out to get her moved in.

"You know I don't think your stuff is going to fit with my bachelor motif. Maybe we should buy some new furniture. Start this little marriage off right."

She gave me a big hug around my neck, "You are just too sweet to me." She kissed me on the lips passionately and before it progressed any further the phone rang.

"Hello Mr. Ray." Maria the housekeeper with her usual greeting. "How was your trip?"

"Oh, it was great. We hated to come back home but we missed you Maria."

"Hello Maria," Viv yelled

"Oh, you so funny. When do you want me to come back?"

"Well you can still take some more time off. Viv and I going to be busy here for a couple of days. I think she wants to redecorate. Didn't you tell me you were going to be helping your husband with a job?"

"Yes I did. I helped him but you know my knees and back aren't young no more. I would rather be doing your laundry or cooking or cleaning toilets than repairing sprinklers, replacing shower heads and fixing broken windows. Maybe I could come over and do your vacation laundry?"

"Ok I get it. Come over tomorrow. We'll find something for you to do. That way you can stop doing sprinkler repairs."

"Oh, thank you so much Mr. Ray, I will be there at 8 a.m. sharp."

"How about 9 a.m. sharp? We're still in honeymoon mode."

"I am so happy you got a good wife."

Thank you Maria, I think I'll keep her. We'll see you tomorrow." I hang up the phone and instantly it rings again.

"Hello?" On the other end was the voice of my law partner Jim Haverty. "Hey buddy next time you go on a honeymoon let me know where you're staying."

"The only next honeymoon will be OUR second honeymoon. Why what's up?"

"I'll tell you what's up, you ever heard of Randy Lockford?"

"Yes, I think anyone that knows anything about sports knows his name. Why?"

"He got a DUI and for some reason he is considering using us."

"My God something like this could put our firm on the map. When is he deciding?"

"He wants to meet with the both of us and get a feel of our professional ability and get this, our looks and personality."

"Will there be a swimsuit or talent portion of the interview?"

"I don't know about that but I do know that he is trying to stay away from the high-profile law firms, he thinks that would just irritate and turn off the general public. His agent agrees and of course I told him that was an excellent strategy."

"Well, I don't know about you but I'm ready to dazzle him, When can we meet with him?"

Suddenly, my day dreaming is brought to an abrupt termination. I hear someone yell out my name, it was then I realize I have driven all the way home and it was one of my neighbors waving and yelling at me. I don't want to talk with any neighbors or anyone else for that matter. When I get out of the car I wave back as I put my head down and make a quick bee line to my front door. I open the door and enter the house. It seems eerily quiet, the feeling of complete emptiness comes over me. I make my way to the kitchen, open the refrigerator and just stand there. It seems the last 24 hours I've have been in one constant blank stare. At that very instant I swear I hear my mom's voice, "You trying to cool down the whole house?" For a minute I swear I smell her oatmeal cookies baking in the oven the thought makes me smile. I take a step back, close the refrigerator along with my youthful past.

"Mr. Ray, I did not hear you come in." My quiet thoughts are broken by Maria." Are you hungry? I fix you something real fast, you go sit and I bring you your drink."

"Maria, the drink part sounds good. I will wait on the eating part."

"Ok. Mr. Ray you go now and I will bring it to you."

I didn't have to be told twice. I head for the Rec. Room even though the doors are still off their hinges and leaning against the hallway walls.

It is my sanctuary. As always I go directly to the aquarium; watching the fish swimming around in the crystal clear water is just as soothing as any cocktail. Viv really did a wonderful job maintaining it. She was the one who took care of the filters, the pumps and keeping the correct water temperature. She choose the fish that would thrive and not eat or kill our existing ones. I couldn't imagine being able to accomplish what she did with the care and expertise. I believe some of these fish have been around a couple of years or more, now that takes conviction, especially with fragile tropical fish.

"I have your drink Mr. Ray," Maria startles me.

"Thanks Maria, just set it over on my desk."

She is such a help to me, she takes care of me and everything from the laundry to shopping. I would be lost without her. I look over at the Grandfather Clock and see it is only a little past 7:00 p.m. It feels like it is much later, I'm just so tired. Tired or not I think it would be best if I give my law partner a call and fill him in on the past 24 hours. I work on my drink while still memorized by the swimming fish. I glance over at the clock when it starts to chime on the quarter hour. I hold up the glass and make a toast, "I will miss you Viv." I let what was left of my vodka tonic slide down my throat ice and all."

I move away from the fish watching and head over to my desk. There I dial up Jim. I wait as the rings mount up and realize I should have tried his cell phone rather than the office phone. I hang up before the answering machine comes on and quickly dial his cell number and get an immediate, "Hello Jim Haverty speaking."

"Hey Jim, Bob here."

"What's up partner?"

"I would sure like it if you came over to the house; I need to talk with you."

"Is everything ok?"

"I will explain it all when you get over here."

"I'm on my way, see you in a few" I could tell by our exchange he hasn't heard a word about Viv's death.

I no sooner I hang up when Maria at the front door, "NO, he doesn't want to come to door. Let the man grieve in peace!"

As I approach the front door I see a young blonde woman with a camera man shining a bright light behind her. I can see some of my neighbors who take their nightly walk with their dogs stopping and gawking. "Mr. Raymonds, Connie Cole with KGGF we would like to talk to you about your wife's death. Do you have a comment?

"Yes. I would like to make a comment. I smile and shut the door on her and her burly camera man."

Through the closed door I hear her, "I'm going to leave my card in case your change your mind. Thank you."

Mr. Ray, I am so sorry. I didn't want you to hear that. They call the house all day, wanted to speak with you. I tell them you are not here or just NO! But they don't listen."

I place one arm around Maria, "Don't worry so much. This will all be over soon."

"Would you like some dinner now Mr. Ray?"

"No thanks Maria, but I would like another drink, it's been a long day for me."

"Si, I understand what you say. I fix you new drink and get your glass when I come back."

"That's fine. Also Mr. Haverty will be dropping by this evening and does not know about Viv's passing, so just show him in and I will tell him."

"That's good. I think it best he hears it from you."

I just sit at my desk with looking at a photo of Viv and me on our wedding day. I move the photo towards the back of the desk but refused to put it in the drawer. I hear the doorbell ring.

"Mr. Ray- Mr. Haverty is here.""

Please show him in. I stand to meet him as he walks into the room, before I can say a word he exclaims," Jesus Christ! What happened here?"

"Well by you asking that question I'm sure you haven't heard and that's why I called you over. An awful lot has happened, it may be best you sit and have Maria bring you a drink." I call for Maria, "would you fix Mr. Haverty a drink? What would you like?"

"Well from the looks of things we got some pretty heavy shit going on here. Oops, sorry Maria. Get me bourbon over and you better make it a double."

"Si Mr. Jim, I be right back."

I make my way over to Jim extending my hand and thanking him for coming right over.

"Why wouldn't I? It's not every day my buddy calls me and asks if I can come right over, so I knew it must be important."

"Yeah, it is and I don't know how soften the shock, so here is.....Viv is dead."

Jim jumps up, "what are you talking about? What do you mean she's dead?"

"Please, sit down and I'll tell you what I know. I pause and call out again, "Maria, we need our drinks."

"Si, Mr. Ray I am right here," she is standing in the busted doorway. I think she must been there for a few minutes waiting for the right moment to walk in?

"Here, let me take the tray, I reach over take the tray which held the drinks and a small stack of cocktail napkins. "You can call it an evening Maria."

"But I will fix you both some food."

"No, Maria, I think we will be drinking our dinner tonight."

"Are you sure Mr. Ray?

"Jim do you want anything to eat?" He holds up his glass, "This is all I need."

"If you change your mind I will be up watching my TV program. Please no bother come and get me. I fix you both something nice. Good night Mr. Ray. Goodnight Mr. Harverty.

Jim doesn't even wait until Maria is out of ear shot before he asks, "Why in God's name you didn't call me? I've been out of town the past few days working on a case. I haven't been keeping up the news. So, start from the beginning. What the hell happened?

"I don't know. I'm still trying to wrap my head around it myself. There are so many questions. The police and the medical examiner have questions of their own."

Jim still standing but has his head down shaking it ever so slightly, "What do you mean police why are they involved. What the hell is going on here?

"Jim please sit down you're making me nervous." He inhales slowly and sits across from me, "How you doing partner? I know you and Viv have been having your struggles the past few months but I know you stilled loved her."

I don't know why but his words hit me hard. I suddenly break down and start to sob. He gets up and puts his hand on my shoulder, "let it out, don't try and hold the sorrow in." We just sit in silence for a moment.

"You'll get through this, you're a strong guy and I will be with you every step of the way." I see humor in his words because no sooner he says that, he walks back towards his drink. After nearly downing it in one motion, he asks, "Do you know how long we have been best of friends?

He gives me no time to answer," I'll tell you just in case you have forgotten, which I know you haven't. We first met in law school."

"Yes, I remember, and even back then we talked about owning our own firm. I get up from my chair and go about the room turning on lamps, even the light by the aquarium. I sit back down I notice Jim had finished his drink and is ready for another. I don't want to bother Maria after telling her she was done for the evening, so I take matters into my own hands and go to the kitchen for new supplies I know Jim well enough to know that two aren't going to cut it. I decide to bring the whole damn bottles along with some ice and mix. When I walk back into the Rec. Room I display my bounty, "are you ready for a long evening?"

"Jim, I think I need to talk, and there is no one I would rather share my soul than with you."

"I appreciate that, and if you want, just take some time away from the office for a while."

"No, I think I need to keep busy, it will help me from dwelling on it. You understand?

"Yeah, I understand completely, but Bob, you got to tell me what happened? Why the cops?" So, I give him the rundown from the time I was notified at the card game until I got home from the police interview. We continue to drink and talk about the old days until we both start slurring our words and dozing off. It was then I realize we weren't as young as we used to be.

I recommend Jim take the guest room, He stumbles a bit has he stands up from the couch. He nods in agreement and we call it a night.

The next morning starts off as usual with the sound of my curtains being pulled open by Maria. I wish she wasn't so consistent, the bright morning light not only makes me squint it makes my head throb.

"Good morning Mr. Ray, how are you feeling?"

"Well to tell you the truth I was doing ok until you opened the curtains."

"Oh, I'm so sorry. I close them and you go back to sleep."

"No, I need to get up and see if Jim wants some breakfast."

"Mr. Jim was leaving when I was coming upstairs, I asked him if I could fix him something to eat and he say coffee to take with him. He also told me to tell you he would be calling you later today."

"I can tell you I won't let your culinary talents go to waste." My heart wanted the food, but my stomach turned over with the thought of it.

"Culinary?"

"What it means is you're a really good cook and I love whatever you fix me."

Maria smiles from ear to ear and blushes with embarrassment. "You take your shower and I have your coffee and breakfast ready when you come downstairs."

"Sounds like a deal." With that we head in our respective directions. Her to the kitchen and me to my special designed master bathroom.

It cost me a small fortune to have it remodeled to my specifications. With its Jacuzzi tub big enough to fit two, walk-in shower with three shower heads to hitting you from every direction, and choice of five different sprays. I get in and feel my hangover headache disappear almost immediately as the warm water hits my face and the back of my neck. As the water envelopes my face, ribs and my entire body I start to think about the conversation Jim and I had last night. He told me things that only large quantities of alcohol could bring out in someone.

My shower done, I decide to see Dr. Radcliff again. I hope he could squeeze me in today, I really needed to work some things out. I take two aspirin out of the medicine cabinet the help with the headache and two TUMS to help with the heartburn in my chest. I get dressed and head downstairs to the aroma of bacon and fresh brewed coffee.

"Do you feel better after your shower, Mr. Ray? You look better." She has a dish cloth over her forearm and a plate with my steaming hot breakfast. She sets it down in front of me as she also pours me my coffee and some orange juice.

"Maria you're worth every penny you get. I really don't know what that is since Viv was the one that set up your salary."

"Oh, don't worry about my pay; Ms. Viv was very generous and put the money in the bank automatically. I don't know how she did that without going to the bank? She a very smart lady, and oh yes, a beautiful room of my own. I couldn't be happier with my job Mr. Ray, Jesus has blessed me.

"Why don't you sit and have some coffee with me?"

"Oh no, I don't drink coffee plus I need to start on my cleaning you just relax." As she starts washing the breakfast dishes and I open the morning paper, I hear the front door chimes.

"Ay di mios! That can't be the news crews so early. When Maria comes back into the kitchen standing right alongside her is my neighbor Larry. A balding, extremely thin weasel of a man. She looks at me and shrugs her shoulders.

"Don't get all upset at your housekeeper, she told me to wait, but I know you would have told her to have me come back later."

"You're right Larry, I'm not in the mood for neighborly conversation so please respect my wishes."

"Yeah, yeah that's what my old lady told me, but I never pay attention to half the shit she tells me."

"Well this time you should have. I'm running late, so why don't you come by later." Just the sound of his voice makes my heart race.

"I just wanted to say I liked your wife and I'm going to miss seeing her around."

"Thanks Larry, that makes me feel better." The idiot seems to miss my sarcastic tone.

"I'll show myself out." I couldn't help but notice he never said he was sorry for my loss or ask how I'm doing. No, it was how he was going to miss her.

I have quick flashback of Viv telling me how Larry gave her the creeps, it seemed like he was always staring at her. One day she was in the backyard sunbathing in her swimsuit and reading some home improvement magazines, and good neighbor Larry as the story goes, comes across our joint backyard lawn, carrying two large drinks. "You look like you could use a drink."

I remember Viv putting him on the spot by asking him how he knew she was out there. He told her some story about trimming his flowers and just happening to see her. This was not the first time she found him looking at her or coming over uninvited for various reasons. We both knew he was infatuated with her, but it would be too hard to prove stalking when he lived right next door. To this day I still don't know what Larry does for a living. His house is as big as mine, he has several large trees and bushes surrounding his home; in fact most of the homes in this gated community are indistinguishable from one another.

I look over at Maria and just shake my head, "what an asshole."

"I don't like that man and he always seemed to irritate Mrs. Ray."

"Yeah, we talked about him on several occasions, enough about him, I'm going to give Dr. Radcliff a call and see if he can work me in for a visit." I go to the Rec. Room to use my desk phone. As I step over the splintered wood my first thought is I have so much to do. I need to take care of Viv's funeral arrangements. I should call a remolding contractor, I can't stand to see the room Viv and I worked so hard on, in this condition. I need to get more information from the Wonder Twin Detectives, get back to work. I want to get some sort of resemblance of normalcy back in my life.

"Maria I'm going into the office for a bit. I will have my cell phone with me, if anything comes up."

She scurries down the hall, wiping her hands on her apron as is her unknowing habit. "Mr. Ray. You don't eat much."

"I'm sorry. I just have a lot I need to do." I couldn't tell her that my hangover made it impossible to think about food."

"Si, I call you if something important happens."

"Thanks." I grab my keys off the table in the entryway, which was no worse for wear from the fire department destruction crew. When I walk out my front door there is still yellow crime tape across my front porch, I rip it apart and crumble it up in my fist. The sight of it upsets me, I thought they had removed all of it. I bring it into the car and through it on the passenger's seat.

No sooner do I turn the ignition and Maria comes running out of the house with the house phone in her hand, "Mr. Ray it's the policia they want to talk with you."

I turn the car off and reach out the window, taking the phone. "Mr. Raymonds this is Detective Andrews, I'm I catching you at a bad time?

"Yes, you kinda of are. I have several errands I need to run."

"My partner and I would like to have you come by and just finish a few things up. Could we meet up today?"

"I said I would call you guys and set a time up to meet. I suppose we can do it today. I'm just pulling out of the driveway now, why don't we meet at my office? It's not far from the police station."

"Yes, that will be fine. We will see you in a half hour or so?"

With a bit of caustic tone, I answer. "I guess I'll run my errands later." I give the phone back to Maria and start the car once more.

"Everything ok?"

"It's perfectly fine. Don't worry. In fact I will be home for dinner tonight make me something delicioso, to make up for me skipping breakfast." She smiles and I watch her slowly disappear in the rearview mirror. I didn't have the heart to tell her that my stomach had turned sour and no amount of TUMS is going to help.

I drive along with no radio or C.D. playing, it was pleasantly quiet, the yellow crime tape in the passenger seat keeps catching my eye; the site of it makes my eyes fill with tears, but I hold them back. I just shake my head perplexed; how did my once happy life go so wrong?

I make a right turn onto Main Street and can see our law offices. An average beige building with the hanging shingle, "Haverty & Raymonds Law Firm. We have private parking in the back for ourselves and our clients. I see Jim's car in his spot, it makes me feel better knowing he is here. I really need some moral support, especially with the Wonder Twins Detectives on their way over.

I come through the back door and seem to startle Jim. "Well, I wasn't expecting to see you today, how is your head?"

"It's been worse. My stomach on the other hand isn't doing so hot. I was going to try and see if my shrink could fit me in but got side tracked. Worked out for the best anyway, the detectives are coming by here to talk with me." No sooner had words come out of my mouth Det. Nick Andrews and Det. Ryan White walk in the front door.

Our receptionist Michelle at the front desk greets them with a perky, "May I help you gentlemen?"

"I've got it Michelle, thank you." I immediately rush to greet the Wonder Twins. I have them follow me over to my desk. I'm taken aback when I see several condolence floral arrangements. As I move them I ask, "can I have Michelle get you anything?"

Det. White answers for them both, "No, we're fine thank you."

I point in the direction of Jim standing by his desk across the room. "This is Jim Haverty, my longtime partner, close friend and one damn fine attorney."

Det. Andrews pulls out small steno pad and looks down at it, "We just have a few questions and a request, we really should have asked these questions when you were down at the station."

"Go ahead what do you need?"

"Well it's the same stuff we need in all cases." You more than most, know that the spouse is almost always the prime suspect."

"Yes, I know that, what do you need from me?"

Det. White cuts right to the chase, "First, were you seeing someone on the outside of your marriage?"

"No. Next question?"

"We need your last few bank statements."

"Yes, I can get that for you in the next couple of days. What else?"

"Do you know if your maid recognized who was calling your wife the day she discovered the body?"

"I have no idea; I never thought it was important at the time."

Finally, Det. Andrews chimes in, "Maybe it isn't? But we must look at everything and everyone, don't you agree? He doesn't wait for a response from me before he asks, "How was the marriage?"

"Whoa, Detectives. Our marriage was like any other. It had its up and downs. Why ask me that question l when you know the answer? I am sure you know about the police being called out on a few occasions for domestic disputes."

I feel like I'm talking with Dr. Radcliffe and I might start spilling my guts, which is never a good idea while being interviewed or interrogated. But I think what the hell, I've nothing to hide.

"Yes the marriage was very good until I screwed it up by putting my job ahead of her. I think even that would have been ok. If I would have shared even a fraction of my time with her, but I didn't. It was my work, always my work. 100% of the time, 24 hours a day, all on that case!"

"What case is that?"

"You've got to be kidding me. You don't remember the headlines when Randy Lockford was arrested for his second D.U.I.?"

"I remember some of the other guys talkin about that. I do remember reading he was drunk and left the scene of an accident. You remember that case Ryan?"

"A little, but to tell you the truth I'm not much of a football fan." "Well I can tell you you're not much of a sports fan, Det. White. Randy Lockford is just about the most famous baseball player on the planet."

"Bob. Maybe we should take a break."

Det. White ignores Jim. "You're telling me you defended this guy and made a real big name for yourself, since he was such a high-profile player."

"You got it- Now I see how you made detective, nothing gets by you".

"I sense a tone of sarcasm, Mr. Raymonds?"

"I apologize I'm not acting very professional, I am under a tremendous amount of stress I remember thinking if we win this case it will put us on the map, we could write our own ticket."

"Well, how did the trial go?" Det. Andrews asks

"Did you see the sign when you came in? Haverty & Raymonds Law Offices. I mean come on; it was front-page news for weeks. It was in just about every newspaper across the country."

"How did this case upset your wife?"

"Are you taking notes or just winging it? I told you I devoted all my time and energy on that case. I thought I was doing it for us and our future but she never saw it that way. She couldn't care less about the fame and fortune, and believe me she told me many times in those words verbatim. You know, not only was she a knockout with the body of a swimsuit model, she was smart and she had a college degree in accounting. I even used her in the case that drove us apart."

"Mr. Raymonds can you think of anyone who might have wanted to hurt your wife?"

Now I know the Detectives are ready to activate your Wonder Twin powers.

I think for a moment and then I just spill it. "Well you have to remember it was the first marriage for both of us and I didn't want to screw it up in any way, so I gave in on any of her requests. I shouldn't say requests plural she only had one."

Wonder Twin #1 Det. Andrews goes first, "and that was?"

"I could not invite "Big Jim" under any circumstances."

"You mean Jim Haverty your law partner?" Wonder Twin #2 Det. White is very curious now.

"No, no. Not my partner Jim Haverty. I'm talking about James "Big Jim" Marshall, the one who introduced us. She told me she had her reasons, so I didn't push it. That was her only demand, that "Big Jim" is nowhere in sight."

Detective Andrews seems to want more about Viv's insistence on the exclusion of Big Jim from the wedding. "Mr. Raymonds, do you think there was some sort of relationship either mutual or unwanted with Mr. Marshall and your wife before you met her?"

"She never talked about him. Only thing she ever said about him was he was as phony as, oh never mind, that's another story."

"And the wedding? How did it go?"

"I don't understand what you mean how did it go? It was a very nice wedding nothing extravagant we just had immediate relatives and a few close friends."

"So, there was no disruption during or after the ceremony? No exes of Mrs. Raymonds? Mr. Marshall did not show up?

"No, he didn't. And no exes either."

"And you don't remember anything out of the ordinary?"

"To tell you the truth, my mind was on not screwing up the day."

"And you think this "Big Jim" character is worth looking into?"

"I don't know. All I do know is that Viv could not stand that guy. And maybe the feeling was mutual. What do you want me to say?"

"Tell us about this big case with the famous baseball player you defended. You said that case caused problems in the marriage?"

Now I feel like telling him, go to the newspaper main office and ask for the archives and look it up, but I don't. I figure the more questions I answer of theirs, the more willing they will be to answer mine.

"It was right after we got married and we were moving stuff into our new place. I gave Viv total control of the house decorating and furnishing anyway she saw fit. Mr. Haverty he is the one who broke the news to me about the possible opportunity to defend Mr. Lockford, shortly after that I received a call from Mr. Lockford's agent."

"And his name was? Det. White asks tapping his pen against his other hand.

"Something like Samuels or Samson, maybe even Simpson. I can't remember just now. Anyway the agent asks if we're interested in defending his client. I tell him that we would give Mr. Lockford our undivided attention. I said we would even hand over our other cases to another firm. Of course we had no intention of doing that if we had other cases. I remember the first time I spoke with Lockford's agent...

"I have to ask. Why would Mr. Lockford go for two unknown lawyers?"

"That's exactly whey he wants you two. If the public sees he has high price defense team, I don't believe they would connect with the jury or any Joe Blow on the street. We don't want them thinking here we go again-money buys freedom. But, if the public sees he is using an unknown firm with fresh, unheard lawyers, they might think he is doesn't need a large big name law firm to get him off because he is innocent of all charges. Do you see what I'm getting at?

"Yes, the way you explain it, you could almost defend him." I flatter in hopes to charm him

Something was a little off about Lockford's agent He tried too hard. I bet he never played sports in his life, but was living vicariously through his client. "What did they charge him with?"

"I will let my client give you the details. I think it's best you hear it from him."

"When is the best time for us to meet Mr. Lockford?" I can't help but think if Jim and I take this case we will have our hands full. "I don't release that Mr. Samson is on some tirade.

"...I also think the newspapers have been known to take sides in cases like this. Just about every time they favor the poor and needy vs. the rich and privileged. Don't you agree Mr. Raymonds?

I don't want to tell Mr. Samson I wasn't listening. I was thinking the prestige this sort of case would bring, so I gamble and just lie. "Yes, I agree."

"The press likes to build our heroes up and then tear them down. I told Rand...." He corrects the slip immediately. "Mr. Lockford if we bring in a defense dream team like they did for O.J. if would backfire. You know what I think?"

He doesn't wait for me to respond.

"All the Juice needed was Johnnie Cochran. He's the one that won over that jury. So one of your hurdles is going to be to find the right jury. It will be up to you to excuse those that show any bias against a wealthy superstar. It is your job to always keep in the back of your mind that this white client has an income that is 20 times more than any juror that you select. And it's my job to make sure that income isn't jeopardy. I'm working on a new endorsement deal. But that's all on the back burner until this little dust up is settled."

I can't believe he is telling me how to handle a case we haven't even agreed to take. "Let's say Mr. Haverty and I take the case. How soon can you set up an appointment with him?"

"This evening should be good. We need to get all our ducks in a row."

I hate that term. It sounds stupid, but I keep that thought to myself. And why does he use the term we?

"You know what I'm getting at Mr. Raymonds?" You and your partner can interview him and ask all the questions you need to. And then decide whether to take the case."

"Give me his address and phone numbers and we will arrange a time."

I'm interrupted by Det. White, "So tell me, you just got married, moving into a new house, remodeling and redecorating and possibly taking on a high-profile case. Don't you think you were biting off more than you could chew?"

"Well in hindsight that might have been true, but at the time I thought it was perfect, not only for my career but for our marriage. Viv had decided to take time off. She was let go by Big Jim and didn't care that much for her new job, so she looked forward to making the house a home. I honestly thought I could manage. But, when we got the file on Mr. Lockford's case, Jim and I knew it was a uphill battle. It was his second DUI, a hit and run and leaving the scene of an accident. My first thought is there is no way we can get him off from all charges, maybe having some reduced was are best hope.

"Randy Lockford wasn't the golden goose you thought he would be for the firm?" Det. White's smirks as he says it.

I come back with, "I don't know why you would say that?"

"He was a household name across the country but here he was hometown hero, a living legend. We had that going for us, or at least I hope we did? After going through the police report, I thought even being a home grown boy wouldn't give us the slightest advantage. I tried to find a silver lining but only saw storm clouds; there were just so much damaging accusations in that report." .....

"Detectives if you want to hear more we could set up another meeting. If I rehash the entire case we will be here all night. I do have other matters that need my attention."

"We will be in touch. Mr. Raymonds." With that Det. Andrews leans over my desk, extends his hand and I shake it. He joins Det. White who is waiting for him at Michelle's desk. I clasp my hands behind my head and roll my chair closer to the wall so I could rest my head. I close my eyes and instantly recall the first time I met Mr. Randy Lockford.

Mr. Lockford wanted to meet at his home and I had to admit to myself I was curious to see how a top notch millionaire ball player lived.

When Jim and I pull up to the address his agent Mr. Samson had given me, I was surprised it wasn't some gaudy mansion with a security fence surrounding it. Instead, Randy Lockford lived on the top floor of a classic hotel in the Heart of the City. Where he like to show off his prosperity, he had the entire 24th floor to himself. And Mr. Samson had told us major renovations had been done per his specific requests. He lived alone, with the exception of his live in houseboy. That was the exact word Mr. Samson had used, 'houseboy'

Jim and I arrive at a gated underground parking lot with access only through an armed security guard. We were only buzzed through after the guard made a call to Lockford and was given consent. We make our way to the elevator and onto the 24th floor. When the elevator opened we step out, only to be two or three feet from a large solid oak door. There was no doorbell but one wasn't needed, the door opened and we were greeted by a young Filipino man dressed in a white coat and black bowtie. He bent slightly at the waist as we entered the spacious vestibule.

I have to ask," How did you know we were at the door?"

He spoke in perfect English, "We have cameras and motion detectors from the underground garage to where you are standing now."

"Mr. Lockford is expecting you. Please follow me." And with that we were led through a beautiful entry way with white marble floors which led onto pure white carpet that looked like it had never been walked on. There were large picture windows looking out over the city, the whole ambiance gave off the distinctly feel of wealth.

"Would you like something to drink?" he asked.

"Oh, no thank you, I'm fine." I look in the direction of Jim and see he is standing at the huge picture windows and was mesmerized by the view. I answer for him, "he's fine, thank you." The 'houseboy' bowed and left the room without making a sound. I walk to where Jim is standing. "Sure, is something isn't it?" Jim didn't answer me he just let out a small sigh. We both turn when we hear Mr. Lockford walk, into the room.

"Thank you for meeting me here." He was wearing a velour sweatshirt that looked like it was made to match his carpet; he was very calm, for a man possibly facing jail time.

"Did Tan offer you something to drink?"

"Yes, thank you, were both fine." I bend over and open my briefcase as Jim and I sit down. I take out a mini recorder, "We are short on time. Would you mind if we tape this conversation, Mr. Lockford?"

"Please, call me Randy. We are going to be spending some time together don't you think we should be on a first-name basis? And I don't mind as long as it doesn't show up on ESPN or in the tabloids."

"Of course not Randy. I am Robert and this is Jim."

"Jim and Bob. My dad used to listen to an old radio show with two comedians named Jim and Bob or was it Jim and Ray?"

I interrupt him. "Why don't we start on what happened from the time the ball game was over, until the time you were arrested, and see if you can remember everything you did, no matter how small or insignificant you may think it is,"

"I will give it to you just as I remember. As soon as the game ended I headed straight to the locker room. See, usually I stop and talk with some fans, sign some stuff, but that night I wasn't feeling it. Not even for lovely ladies that usually wait around."

"And why was that?" I continue to take notes.

"Jesus, I couldn't find my rhythm that night. Don't know if you guys are baseball fans, but I struck out twice. And if that wasn't enough, I made a throwing error that let in two runs, costing us the game. I was in no mood to see anyone. Not the fans, not the ladies and sure as shit-not the hecklers."

"What happened when you got to the clubhouse, anything out of the ordinary?" Jim asked.

"Nope the team was decompressing and waiting for our coach to give permission for the press to come in. You know, come to think of it, there was something out of the usual. The coach came up to me and asked if I wanted him to keep the press at bay."

"He'd never asked that before?"

"No and believe me, I had shitty games before. I told him I'm a big boy and I can handle it, so I grabbed a beer and waited at my locker for the press to come in and ask their usual stupid questions. Randy demonstrates with a mocking tone. So Randy did you have a hangover tonight? Stay out too late? What's the reason for the bad game?"

Jim stops the recorder, "You said you had a beer, just one?"

"Yeah, I guess. I don't know. After the press left Jake..."

"Who's Jake?"

"He's the clubhouse manager who takes care of us. He calls us 'his boys'. He brings us sandwiches, beers, sodas. Whatever we might need."

"What do you mean by whatever?"

"No, no. It's not like that. I don't do pills, or steroids or anything of that shit. I like a beer after the game. And that's it!"

Jim and I look at each other. He turns the recorder back on.

"I do remember him asking if anyone wanted another soda or beer before he dumped out the ice from the cooler. So, yeah, I think I might have had one more?" Randy started to get nervous; he walked over to the wet bar nestled against the wall and reached into a small refrigerator and grabbed a soda.

He blurted out. "Hey, you know now that I think about it, I didn't finish that second beer I took one more swig then tossed it in the garbage."

"How much would you say was left in it?"

"I don't know for sure, but I would say way more than half."

Randy comes and sits back down in front of us."

"So you leave the park. Anyone see you?"

"There were a couple of hanger ons but I keep my head down, get in my car and head home."

"Well if that was true we wouldn't be here would we? Something happened and we want to hear it from you, don't leave anything out."

"Yeah, I got it." He takes a sip from his soda can.

"I don't think you do. This is a serious situation you are in, we are not talking about a meager fine, were talking prison time."

"Your right, I guess I'm in denial. I don't even want to think what could happen. I'll give it to you straight, nothing left out." He finishes off the last remnants of his soda, squeezes the can and leaves it on the coffee table. "I headed home and everything was cool until I got to the intersection of Grant Ave. and Ordway St. I had the red light so I slow down and stop before the crosswalk line. As I'm sittin there lookin around, I notice this guy standing by the light pole,

"What made you notice him?" I ask.

"I don't know? I just think to myself, he's going to step off that curb, start walking across the street and he isn't going to make it before the light changes. I looked in my rearview mirror to see if more cars were coming, because he's not paying attention and sure as shit, I bet he's gonna get creamed."

"And were there any cars in either direction?"

"No, but it don't matter really. See he takes about three steps and goes back to the signal control and pushes the cross walk button and stays put, so I figure I don't have to worry him. Now my light is green and I give it the gas to be on my way."

"Do you know what time this was?"

"I say 11:30, maybe midnight."

"Ok go on."

"Well, like I said the light is green and I'm crossing into intersection, the next thing I know out of nowhere my head lights reflect off a car in front of me and Bam!"

"Did you try and slow down?"

"I hit the brakes but it was way too late, the collision was right into the passenger's side of the other car. My airbag deploys and I can't see a thing.

"Did you get out of the car?"

"Yeah, as soon as my head clears and I realize what just happened. I feel a little groggy, but no blood or broken bones that I know of. I go check on the other car and see if everyone is ok.

"And were they?"

"The driver said he was fine. But then I heard crying and looked in the back seat and see two young kids."

"Did they look like they were hurt?"

"They looked upset and frightened, but no. I didn't see any blood, but the passenger windows are shattered. I tell them to hold on I'm going to call for help. That's when the driver gets out and starts speaking in Spanish."

"Did you understand what he as saying?"

"Some of it. He was waving his hands and kept saying "we ok, we ok. Please senor. Then I realize there is a woman in the passenger side, she looks pretty shook up but not hurt in any way that I can see, I thank God I didn't pick up speed from my light. The passenger door is crushed in. I try to get it open.

"Did she say anything?"

"No, the guy is still just saying, we ok, we ok... So he gets back in the car and they take off. I can't believe it, I look over in the direction of the man waiting to cross the street and ask him, "Have you ever seen anything like that?" He just shrugs his shoulders and shakes his head no and throws his cigarette on the sidewalk

"Did you call for help?"

"No, I look at my car and there's very little damage. I was ok and they must have been okay, because they left and that's what I did. I didn't need the press finding out about it."

"You left the scene and didn't call anyone?"

"I just wanted to get home, but I didn't get far! Made it a few blocks before I had to pull over. I started shaking. Must have been a delayed reaction of what could have been a disaster. I may have been in shock."

"Could be possible. Or you could have had a head injury." Jim will need to get some expert witnesses for that. Continue Randy."

"So, put my head down on the steering wheel and said a short prayer, which was out of the ordinary, due to the fact I'm not much of a religious person. But I had to thank God no one was hurt. The next thing I know someone was tapping on my window. I look up to see a blinding light. I lower the window a bit and I see it's a cop."

I look at the file, "That would be Officer Spencer."

He asked what seems to be the problem. So I tell him I was in a fender bender but I'm fine. Next thing I know he tells me to step out of the car.

"Did you get out of the car?"

"NO! I ask why? I wasn't doing anything wrong."

That's when he started acting like a real prick. Tells me I left the scene of an accident. Asks me if I had been drinking.

"And what did you tell him?"

"What everyone says, I had one maybe two."

In an arrogant tone Randy mimics the policeman. I will be the judge of that. Now get out of the car. I will be conducting a roadside sobriety test, sir.

"And did you take the test?"

"Well, not exactly." I get out of my car and give it to him straight, I tell him I'm shaky from the accident and show him the deployed airbag. I try to tell him the other party just took off. Didn't give me a chance to give any info." So, you know what he does?" He put's my hands behind my back, cuffs me and says, you're under arrest.

Next thing, he is lowering my head and putting me in the squad car. And that asshole pushes down real hard causing a sharp pain in my neck. I yell, "What the fuck is your problem?"

No words were spoken during the ride to the station"

"Tell me "Mr. Lockford?

"Remember, call me Randy."

"Randy, did they ask you needed medical attention."

"Sure as shit did not!"

"Do you remember taking a breathalyzer test?"

"Oh yeah, they did that right after they finger printed me."

"Wait a minute." I look over at Jim.

He asks Randy," are you sure the finger printing came before the breathalyzer."

"Yes I'm sure, because I was still wiping the ink off my hands when they asked me to blow into the tube."

"Did you see the reading?"

"No, but the guy giving me the test told me the machine was acting up and needed to get a different one. I remember because I cussed at him about needing a different one because they didn't like the results they're getting on that one? He looked up at me like he got caught with his hand in the cookie jar. He grabbed the machine and headed off across the room. But I did notice him going into the Chief's office. The next thing I know the tester is telling me I'm free to go. I don't ask any questions I just take off."

"If everything you say is even close to what happened, I believe we will have a very good chance to have all charges dropped. Tomorrow we will subpoena all the paperwork involved with your arrest. After we do that we will give you a call and go over our findings. I think we will try and find that eye witness. We might need his testimony. Do you remember what he looked like?"

"Skinny dude, greasy hair. I don't know. He looked average."

"I think that's enough for tonight, Randy." We shake Randy's hand and Mr. Tan shows us out.

In the parking garage Jim and I come up with our plan of attack.

"Jim, you get the police reports first thing tomorrow and make sure to get a copy of the breathalyzer results and the tester's name. I will see if I can find that witness, he saw the whole accident and Randy talked to him.

If you call a shrug of the shoulder a conversation. That's not going to be easy Bob. Especially with the great description Randy gave."

"Nothing ever is. But I bet there are surveillance cameras somewhere near that intersection." We do a slight bounce as we reach the car.

"So this is how the other half live, Bob?"

"No Jim- I think this is how the other 5% live."

The first thing I want to do, is share the great news with Viv. I look at my watch, it's late, 11pm but I'm just too excited. I call her on the cell as soon as I drop Jim off at his house. She answers concerned, "where are you? Are you ok?"

"Yes, I am fine, I have some good news and I want to tell you in person. Meet me at OUR restaurant'."

"Let me change and I will be there ASAP." I always felt the two of us were like the classic movie characters from the forties film, The Thin Man, minus the smart little dog. While I waited at the bar I asked the bartender if dinner is still being served, unfortunately it stopped at eleven. After sipping on my drink for twenty minutes or so Viv taps me on the shoulder. I turn around and instantly give her a passionate kiss.

"Wow!" She wipes her lipstick from my mouth. "I guess the meeting went well?"

"Viv, this case is going to put the firm in the black for years! We got a very rich client, who was treated very poorly by the police. I think Jim and I might even have a civil case against the Police Department."

"Bob that seems like an awful big undertaking for a firm just starting out."

I flag the bartender down. "We'd like some champagne please."

"I will have to go in back to get it. It will take a moment."

"No problem, we are celebrating tonight." I lean over to kiss Viv again, but I can tell she is tense. "What. What is it Viv?"

"Nothing, I'm happy for you."

"You mean for us?"

"Yes, Bob for us. It's just..." She doesn't finish the thought. The bartender comes back with the champagne and pops the cork.

I try to change her mood with a toast, "Do the start of a beautiful friendship."

She smiles, "we're married. I think it's more than a friendship." We clink our glasses together.

"I just don't think you comprehend the enormous possibilities this case is going to bring us."

"Enormous RESPONSIBITIES...Bob! This case sounds like it is going to require a lot on your time. I just thought our honeymoon phase would last a little longer."

I lean in closer to her and whisper in her ear, "We will always be in the honeymoon phase."

We sit and talk until they came to tell us it was closing time. I tip the piano player a $20 to play one more song; the 1977 pop/country hit, "Don't It Make My Brown Eyes Blues." That was the last time Viv and I danced.

I am jolted awake and almost fall off my desk chair at the loud knock on my desk. "I thought I would give you some quiet after the detectives left. How you holding up?

"Jim I need some work. I've been reminiscing a lot and I need to focus on anything else. You got a case?"

"You want a case partner?"

"Yes, that is exactly what I want. You know I'm still paying those doctor bills"

"Well, I do have one case. Mind you it's no Supreme Court case, but it could occupy your thoughts."

"I'll take it. I don't care if it's jaywalking," Jim gives me the case file which I decide to look over at home. When I hop in my car I look at myself in the rearview mirror. I don't recognize myself. I'm pale and look tired with dark circles. I rub my eyes and turn on the radio in an effort to wake up. And there it is, I hardly believe my ears, coming through the speakers was the subtle sound of the female voice singing... Don't know when I've been so blue, don't know what's comer over you. You found someone new. And don't it make my brown eyes blue.

I don't know if it was the song or my weariness, but my mind started playing its own private movie screening of some of the toughest and lowest points in my life. One such occasion I remember coming home from work tired and a little irritated, asking her...

"Viv, where have you been? I've been calling all day. She doesn't answer me. I follow as she continues upstairs. "Viv?"

She starts to undress. "What does it matter?"

"I would like to know!"

"No, you don't!"

"We can't go on like this!" She says nothing and shuts the door to the bathroom. I don't know what made Viv change. At first she was sullen and withdrawn, that gave way to anger and hostility. Whatever the cause, our marriage disintegrated at a rapid pace. I thought we were happy but I must have been blind or just didn't want to know. Once the numerous affairs started, she moved out of the master bedroom. We could go days with speaking to one another. Maria was our go between.

My dreams began sporadically at first. I would wrap my hands around her throat and squeeze. She would squirm and try and tear at my face, but I held on. Her face would turn red and my bare hands would squeeze harder. Until...

Dr. Radcliff is right. I am under a lot of stress. I loved Vivian and I know I couldn't have done anything to hurt her. I must keep focused and nothing says focus like the law.

Maria has dinner waiting for me when I get home. "Maria can you bring it into the Rec. Room? I have a case I want to look over."

"Oh, of course Mr. Ray."

I read the file Jim gave me. The client is Alex Fontain. The charges were failure to comply with a restraining order and stalking charges. I call Jim and ask if he can add anything to the file. "He says he's innocent, Bob."

"Aren't they all?"

"He says they are bogus charges, his ex- wife's boyfriend is telling her what to say when contacting the police. Get this? He's a cop."

"A cop?" Maria gently knocks on the half open door. I wave her in.

"Mr. Fontain can fill you in when you see him; I set up an appointment for tomorrow around one thirty, but don't stress out, in my opinion I think you've got a good chance to get it thrown out. I predict it won't go to trial."

"That would be fine with me. See you tomorrow."

That night I have a much different dream. Viv is at some sort of party, surrounded by men. Some I know, like "Big Jim", Randy Lockford, the bartender from that night at the restaurant. Others I either don't know or can't see their faces. Viv is laughing, but then the circle of men is pushing in on her. Their hands forcing her to the ground and their laughing turns to screaming. I try to reach her...BUT

I wake up to Maria opening the shutters in the Rec. Room. I have spent the entire night in my Recliner Chair with the Fontain file on my lap. I start to wonder about my health. Could I have narcolepsy?

"You okay Mr. Ray? You are sweating?"

"I'm fine. Just a restless night."

"You hungry?"

"No, nothing for me. I am very anxious to get into the office. I put the files in my briefcase. "I'm going take a quick shower. I will see you tonight."

She just looks at me with concern and worry. "Always running, always in a hurry, you slow down and drive careful."

"Yeah. Yeah, drive careful." As I head upstairs I think of the Beatles with their mop top hair singing 'yeah, yeah, and yeah'. Better to think of the Fab Four, than of any of that awful nightmare.

When I get to the office I'm primed and ready to go. Michelle our receptionist is coming in late due to a dentist appointment. I hang up my jacket, sit in my swivel chair behind my desk and come to a stop. I take notice of the little red light flashing on my phone, taunting me. I push the button. I have three messages, "Mr. Ray, it is Maria" with her thick accent. "The police say they are coming to the house 5 p.m. They want you here and me too."

Poor Maria, she worries so much, most of all about me. I call her back but the house message machine kicks on. "Maria I will be home before 5 and I will handle the police. Please don't worry."

I play the next message it's a sales call. The last message is from my new client, Alex Fontain. "Mr. Raymonds I was told you would be handling my case and I know Mr. Haverty set up an appointment for 1:30, but the thing is I need to push it to 2:00, maybe 2:30. Please call me back." I write down his number, but before I can return his call, my phone rings. I answer like I haven't in years. "Good morning, Haverty and Raymonds, Mr. Raymonds speaking."

"Oh good you're the man I wanted to speak with, this is Alex Fontain. I wanted to make sure you got my message about pushing our meeting later?"

"No problem, Mr. Fontain. I will see you between 2-2:30pm." I hang up the phone and take a half turn in my swivel chair. I am somewhat surprised to see Jim get up from his desk and head's towards me.

"Hey, have you eaten yet?" Jim asks.

"I even know you were here. You were quiet has a church mouse, back there in your corner of the world. No, I haven't eaten. Maybe I should have something in my stomach. I haven't eaten since sometime last night."

"Great, I'll fly- If you buy."

"Deal. I'll take the usual, salami and swiss, no tomatoes and a bag of chips. I get my wallet out and hand him a $20. Jim gives a salute, does a little quarter twist on the heels of his of his shoes and heads out the door. I keep myself busy with the Fontain file, until I hear- "lunch is here!"

Jim walks in his hand full of sandwiches and chip bags. The sight of the lunch makes my stomach growl. I spread out the napkins over my desk and I demolish the food.

"You must have been hungry?"

"I guess so." I wipe my mouth and chin. Michelle is back from the dentist and buzzes the intercom.

"A Mr. Fontain is waiting to see you."

I look at my watch. He is early. I throw the lunch wraps into the waste basket. "Ok, send him in." I sit up straight in my chair and try to give the air of professionalism. I stand and offer my hand to shake. Hello I'm Bob, Bob Raymonds and this is Jim Haverty."

"Hi, I'm Alex Fontain." He is a big man and holds his hand shake a little longer than customary. I gestured for him to take a seat.

He sits and replies, "I am so glad you decided to take my case.

"No problem, but I'm sorry I thought you were running late."

"'I finished early, I hope that won't be a problem?"

"No, we are just finishing up a very important case, hungry v. lunch."

Jim takes the rest of the chips, "I will leave you two discuss the case."

I grab a legal pad. "Let's start with you telling me your side."

"Yeah that would be great. I want this thing settled as soon as possible. As far as I'm concerned, it's a bunch of bullshit! My ex hates my guts and wants to put me through hell. I know for sure she set me up, causing this violation of the restraining order."

"Tell me how she has been setting you up?" I listened as I look him over. He's in his mid-forties, well-groomed, wearing blue jeans and a nice short sleeve shirt. He looks like a regular working stiff and I bet his wife is trying to screw him over for everything he ever owned. I listen as he lays out his story. I watch his body language, trying to see if it gives any clues. Most lawyers multitask, being able to read your client, because the prosecution and the judge sure are. "So, your wife called you and told you to get all of your stuff out of the garage?"

"Yes."

"Did she call you at home or on your cell?"

"On the cell when I was at work."

"That's good news."

Michelle buzzes the intercom again. "Mr. Raymonds line one. It sounds important."

"Excuse me Mr. Fontain."

Immediately, I know something is wrong. Maria is frantic, "Mr. Ray! The police are hear. They want to talk to me. What do I do?"

"I'm on my way. Tell them you are waiting for your attorney, abogado, attorney Maria! I hang up.

"Mr. Fontain, I'm sorry but I must leave. Please talk to Michelle and we can arrange another appointment. Again I'm so sorry."

"Sure, but before you go, tell me if you think I have a good case?"

"Yes, I think we do, from what you've told me. I will be able to give you a more definitive answer after I investigate a few things. But as it stands now, it looks promising."

"Thank you, I hope everything is alright?"

After shaking hands I take the back door to my car. I don't have time to explain to Jim... I drive faster than the speed limit, crossing my fingers I don't get pulled over. I know the detectives are just doing their job, but what reason to talk to Maria without me present? I know investigators won't find a connection involving me with Viv's death. But it seems I'm the only suspect they have. They don't seem to be looking for any others. They must not know that Vivian stepped on a lot of people in her short life. She had countless lovers she dropped without much concern for their feelings and I know how that felt first hand. I loved her more than anything and she treated me like shit. I would have to rehash our whole bloody business with the detectives.

Before I know it I'm pulling into my gated community. I shake my head out of the past and into the present. I enter the code for the gate and it begins to swing open; I drive the short distance and pull into my driveway. There are two cars in front of my house. An unmarked police car and a squad car with a young Latina officer standing next to it.

As I enter the house, Maria jumps off the couch where the Wonder Twin Detectives are also sitting. ""Gracias, Mr. Ray." She is wringing her hands.

I pat her gently on the shoulder and look her in the eyes and whisper, "don't worry, Maria." I tell her again in my best Spanish, "no te procupes, Maria."

"Hello detectives? Can I offer you something to drink?" I already know the answer.

"No Mr. Raymond, we are on duty."

"Of course. Maria why don't you bring some of those nice cheesy crackers for the detectives? Well let me see if I can't get it straight. I point my index finger to the right with my thumb up resembling a gun. Det. White and Det. Andrews, I could have sworn we did not have an arranged appointment or am I mistaken?"

"We were in the neighborhood and had a few questions for Mrs. Sanchez."

"Of course you were. And the young officer outside my door? Not to stereotype, but I bet she speaks fluent Spanish?"

"Well I must say you're quite the observant one. I hope you were as observant the afternoon your wife died. Do you know anyone who would want to hurt your wife?"

"Yeah, I can think of some people, if I knew any of their names. In fact, I doubt she even knew half their names…if you know what I'm getting at?"

"Your wife was unfaithful."

"That sums it up."

"So that must have made you very angry?"

"Not enough to kill her. But I can't say the same for those she stepped on. She had a way of making a man feel special, like they were the only one. They would wine and dine her, shower her with luxurious gifts, those who could afford it, and when she was done, she was done!! She could not only break their hearts and their spirts, but also their bank accounts."

"And you were aware of all these affairs, Mr. Raymonds?" Det Andrews asks.

"I'm not blind or stupid. I don't expect you to understand our relationship. Shit! I didn't understand it. I would start with some of her cast offs, you may find someone who would want to harm her."

"Can you give us a name to start with?"

"I have no idea who they were or they came from. And I didn't want to know. Look I would help you if I could. I want to know what happened to my wife. No one will tell me how she even died."

"Mr. Raymonds this is an ongoing investigation. We are in the business of asking questions."

"It's a simple question. What was listed as the cause of death?" Detective White takes the lead. "The official cause of death was a puncture wound into the heart."

"You mean she was stabbed to death?"

"No-That's not accurate. The doctor who performed the autopsy could not say for sure it was a puncture wound from any weapon he could determine. The entry wound had no jagged edge or tear and the wound was found only on the body, not through the clothes."

"I don't understand. I am considered a good lawyer and a fairly smart man, but I can't fathom what you telling me."

"Mr. Raymonds there is a theory though not considered very solid, that the injury or wound was caused by an implosion in her chest and may have been from natural causes. Tests are still being conducted."

"Whoa, hold on! Are you telling me there might be a chance my wife was not murdered at all?"

Detective White was becoming impatient. "That's not what Detective Andrews is saying at all! What we're saying is at this point the cause of death is a puncture wound to the heart. We are trying to determine is what caused it."

Detective Andrews tries to change the topic, "Our department is in full swing. We are checking out all Vivian's acquaintances.

"Detectives let me tell you, Vivian didn't have close friends of any kind!"

"We are looking for the ones who might have resented sharing her affection with others."

"You mean like me? You got to be kidding. "Listen, I had all but given up on her infidelity but we had come to an agreement."

"What kind of agreement?" "She would keep her affairs out of this house. I didn't want to see it, or hear about it!"

Det. Andrews nods like he feels sorry for me, "I was hoping deep in my heart she would get this out of her system and we could reconnect like we did in the beginning."

I was getting frustrated. I hated that I had to air my 'dirty laundry'. I hate that they thought ill of my dead wife.

"I don't disagree that there were times I hated her! I wanted her dead. She put me through Hell! I was depressed. I couldn't eat. I couldn't sleep! And when I did, I had terrible dreams. Dreams where I watched her die. But I don't think on my worst day I could..."

Maria came in the room in a rush with a plate of cheese and crackers, "Would any one like some coffee? I could make..."

"Pardon me Mr. Raymond, would you like to have a lawyer present?"

Detective White was baiting me. What had I said? I wasn't hanging myself was I? "No! I don't think that will be necessary. I am a lawyer. I know what I can and cannot answer." I told myself I'm in control of this questioning. "Go ahead with your questions I will answer what I can."

"Can you repeat what you just said?"

"And that was?"

"About watching her die? Mr. Raymonds to you think it is possible that you killed your wife in a jealous rage and have blocked it out?"

After hearing that question, it's apparent I should stop talking. I am definitely not in control of this questioning. I pause to consider my answer. "That is a question I can't answer."

"Can't or won't?" Det. Andrews asks.

"Look, all I can say, is I'm seeing a doctor about my past relationship with Vivian. I loved her. No one says anything. Not me, the detectives or Maria. I finally break the tension. "I think that's enough for tonight. I gave you way more time then you deserve without an appointment. We can continue another day. Can I show you guys out?"

"We still have some questions for Mrs. Sanchez." Det. White isn't budging.

"I think that can wait for another day, don't you?"

"That's fine Mr. Raymonds. We will set up a real appointment. But this time I would like you and Mrs. Sanchez to come down to the station."

"Yes, that will be no problem." I look at Maria and she's as white as a ghost.

I walk them to the front door in an effort to conclude this unscheduled meeting. Det. White walks out but Det. Andrews stops in the doorway. "Thank you. We will be in touch. And if you please don't..."

I interrupt before he can finish his statement, "I know. Don't leave town."

Maria is frantic. As soon as I close the front door she blurts out, "Mr. Ray, This is bad?"

"Maria, everything is fine. It's not bad. The detectives are just doing their job."

Maria isn't buying it. "But..."

I change the subject immediately. "Why don't we have a drink?"

"Si, I will make you a drink."

"No, WE have a drink."

As we make our way back to the kitchen area I can't help and think how well had that just gone? Did I come off as smug? Did I say too much?

I pour us two stiff drinks. Maria and I sit at the kitchen table. I down my vodka, Maria twists her glass on the table, never even picking it up. I get up to make another for myself, a little bit stronger this time. "Maria, what else do you remember about the Mrs. Raymonds died?"

She takes a tiny sip from her glass. "Mr. Ray that day starts out the same as all the others. You know how she was"

Maria gets up and throws her drink down the kitchen sink.

"What you didn't like the drink I made you?" I joke.

"Mr. Ray I really don't like alcohol."

"Are you more of a beer girl?"

She busies herself wiping down the counters. "Maria tell me about that day. Anything little detail might help."

"Like I say. She did the same thing every day. She would get the mail, get her reading glasses, fix her drink, just like you; vodka and tonic. Then she goes to Rec. Room. She would lock herself inside and do whatever she does for many hours."

"What did you think she did?" Maria shrugged her shoulders. "I don't know, maybe she reads, drinks or maybe she take siesta?"

"So, you had no idea?"

"No Mr. Ray. Every time she would go in there she would say, Remember Maria, I want quiet and that means no phone calls. "I tell her I know Mrs. Ray."

"Did she always lock the door? Did you ever ask why?"

"Heavens no, Mr. Ray- that is none of my business. I think she just wanted to be alone."

"You don't need lock yourself in a room to be alone. Or could she have been afraid of something or someone?" I whisper. "And what about this man on the phone that day/"

"Mrs. Ray always would come out after a couple of hours, but that day she got a phone call from a very angry man asking to speak with her."

"Who was it!?" My harsh tone stops Maria's cleaning.

"I don't know Mr. Ray. I told him she is not available, but he got very mad and told me it was very important. I looked at the clock and realized Mrs. Ray should have been out of Rec. Room by now.

"And?!" Maria is resistant. "I know talking about that day is difficult but this could be very important Maria?"

"I told him to hold please. I knock on the door and told her there was a man on the phone who say he needs to talk to her right now, he say it is important. But she did not answer. I knock harder and call out her name. I put my ear to the door, I hear nothing. I tried turning doorknob, but of course it's locked."

"Then what happened?"

"I have bad feeling. Things are not right. I'm getting scared. I run around to the side of the house and look in the door windows and see her lying on the couch. I knock on the glass so hard I think it was going to break it. She does not move. I pray to Virgin Mary and run back into the house. The man isn't on the phone anymore so I call 911. I don't remember much after that, sirens, lots of emergency people running and banging on the door. I get out of the way. I didn't know what to do. I have no way to call you. They make me leave house and I don't have my cell phone. I'm so sorry Mr. Ray." I see she is visible upset talking about it.

"Maria, you did everything just right. You don't have to worry. No one could have done anything better than you did." I gently put my hand on her shoulder.

"Do you remember if you told any of the officers about the phone call that night?"

"No. I forgot all about it until we talk tonight. "Do you think the man on the phone is important?"

"Tell you the truth I don't know. Could have been one of Mrs. Raymonds 'associates'." I know Maria isn't naive when it came to Viv and her men, but I have no intention of having that awkward conversation. "I'll let the Wonder Twins know about it."

"Who?" Maria wasn't up on 70s pop culture.

"The detectives from today, Det. White and Det. Andrews. They can look through the phone records and see who called that night. I will call them tomorrow. We've gone through enough for one day."

"Mr. Ray you haven't eaten dinner. Please let me fix you something to eat."

"It's not necessary. You go get some sleep. I will see you tomorrow." I left the kitchen before she could argue. I go upstairs with my briefcase and prop up the pillows near the head board and lean back. I try to close my eyes but my mind is racing. A phone call? A phone call from a man? Could it have been from Randy Lockford? I recall the not so pleasant phone call I had from him...

"Mr. Raymonds I don't care what your wife is saying. All I know is you send her over with some important papers and the next thing I know, Tan is telling me some of my shit is missing. Some of my most valuable awards."

"Mr. Lockford. I assure you that Mrs. Raymonds nor do I have any need for your sports memorabilia,"

"Look I'm grateful for you and Mr. Haverty for doing all you did with my case against the police. But my shit is still missing!"

When I wake up and my body is stiff. This is what happens falling asleep with your head propped up against the head board and not moving from that position during the night. I shower and shave; as I look in the mirror, I think I've aged 10 years. The wonderful scent of bacon and coffee fill the house.

I'm greeted with a very friendly, "Buenos Dias Mr. Ray." Maria is preparing a fabulous breakfast of eggs, bacon, potatoes and the all-important coffee.

"Good morning Maria. Everything looks and smells delicious you can start me off with a cup a coffee? I have a phone call I need to make in the Rec. Room. I'll come out for the rest when I'm done.

"Are you feeling ok today?"

"I think so. I'm ready to slay the dragons."

"Slay demons?"

I chuckle. "Never mind."

I sit behind my desk and phone Dr. Ratcliff's office. I get his exchange service and ask for a Skype session. We've never done one before but I don't have time to go in. They tell me how to set my computer for the Skype appointment. Next thing I know I hear and see Dr. Ratcliff, sweater and all.

In his usual mellow tone, "Good Morning Bob. How are we doing today?"

"WE are not doing so well. I've become so discombobulated. I'm not sleeping. And since you have the degree on the wall."

"Several degrees, thank you."

"Doc, can a person become preoccupied with the past?"

He pauses a moment. "It is quite natural for someone to look back to a time when their life was less complicated. Especially in times of great stress, it is a coping mechanism. Why do you ask?"

"I keep remembering all sorts of different times in my life with Viv. Some are good, some are bad."

"Your mind is trying to come to terms with no only Viv's death, but the mix feelings you had about your marriage. These feelings manifest in your subconscious which transpire in dreams. It is very normal."

"Do you know the cops are questioning me?"

"Bob, you're a lawyer. You know as well as I, that the spouse is always a suspect."

"Suspect in what? They don't have a definitive cause of death. Between my prior dreams and my flashback trips of lately, MAYBE I had some sort of psychotic break and blocked it out. It's possible right?"

"Bob, hitting the lottery or getting struck by lightning is also possible."

"Doc, I didn't hit the lottery and Viv was not killed by lightning."

"It is very unlikely with everything I know about you. Your personality, your personal beliefs. The fact that you never once gave up on your marriage. It doesn't add up."

"You might have to testify to that in court. I mean with no prove of suicide the cops are... But with no known weapon found in..."

"Dr. Radcliff stops my emotional spiral, "would you like to come in today?"

"No, this helped. I will call when I need another pep talk."

"Any time Bob."

I hang up with the doctor and just about to go get my breakfast when the house phone rings, "I'll get it Maria. Hello?"

A young woman with a slight Asian accent is in the other end. "Hello, this is Clean Rite Cleaners. We wanted to tell you that your jacket is ready for pick up. Unfortunately we were unable to remove the stain on the sleeve. We would like to offer you a $10 coupon off your next visit."

"Oh, sure. I will let my housekeeper know."

Maria must have heard I was off the phone, she has plated my breakfast and kept it in the oven to keep warm.

"Maria that was excelente. I ate so much I want to go back to bed. But I most go to work and slay those demons."

When I walk in to the office, Michelle tells me Mr. Fontain is waiting for me. He is sitting in the chair located directly in front of my desk. He stands up as I walk in. "I'm sorry Mr. Fontain. Did we have an appointment today?" I walk to my desk, my facial expression show my confusion. "I don't have it down in my books."

"No Mr. Raymonds, I didn't have an appointment. I need to ask you a question." I settled in my chair and motioned for Mr. Fontain to sit back down. "Sorry, I should have discussed this with you yesterday. I am going to need a ballpark figure on how much you think this is going to cost. I need to know if I can afford your services."

"Of course, Mr. Fontain." First can I offer you some coffee?"

"No, I'm fine, Thank you."

"I will be straightforward with you Mr. Fontain. I don't think this situation between you and your ex-wife amounts to a hill of beans and I hope we can wrap this whole thing in just a couple of days."

With fingers demonstrating air quotes, "and how much will these couple of days cost me?"

"Our rate is $125 an hour. I scribble some figures on a legal pad. "Best estimate of $2500 with a retainer of half... So, $1,250 to start and I will give you a call if it looks like it's going to be more. I'm sure we can work out some arrangement."

"That seems fair, I guess?... I was just concerned." He seems to squirm in his seat. "You've done some very high profile cases."

"Yes, but that was all in the past."

"I remember the Randy Lockford/Police case that told me a lot."

"I appreciate your confidence Mr. Fontain and I will do everything in my power to resolve this as quickly as possible." I stand and hold my hand out, hoping he will take the cue that it's time to leave. Mr. Fontain shakes my hand has he stands, but doesn't let go. I pull my hand away and walk him to the door. "Just one more thing Mr. Fontain."

"You can call me Alex."

"Alex I'm going to need your cell phone. In fact, I might need it for a few days."

"No problem." He reaches to his side and takes it out of a leather case that is clipped to his belt. He hands it to me. "Keep it as long as you need, I don't get many calls."

"I will return it as soon as possible. "Thank you." After he leaves I tell Michelle to hold my calls. Alone at my desk I rummage through the file cabinets preparing myself to battle for Alex. I know this case isn't going to be in the papers. There is no big story line, no WOW factor to capture the media's attention. This is just a case of a Regular Joe who needs help.

I have contections with a previous client who owes me a favor. R.W. is a wizard at getting (hacking) information that would, through proper channels take weeks.

I'm almost 100% sure Mr. Fountain's ex-wife had set him up. I would bet money she would call the poor innocent bastard and tell him to come over and pick up his stuff, and then she would call the police and tell them he is violating the restraining order. I think with the call coming from either the ex's cell, home phone or even by a friend- we could nail her. She would have a hard time explaining that. I'm pretty sure she is calling him at work and we could have one of his coworkers testify to that. I could bluff with the phone records. Make her think I have damning evidence, settle out of court. Turn the tables, get her for harassment and filing a false police report. It all comes down to phone calls. "Phone calls!" I pick up the desk phone and call Det. White.

"Detective White here."

"Detective. It's Robert Raymonds. Listen I don't think it will be necessary for you to speak with Mrs. Sanchez. She told me everything and the most important thing is a strange phone call Vivian received that afternoon."

"Is that so Mr. Raymonds? Well, as you know, we police like to speak with witnesses just to be on the safe side. You understand, of course?"

"But..." He doesn't let me finish.

"We would like you to come in and take a lie-detector test. That's won't be a problem will it?

"You know detective those tests aren't immiscible in court?"

"So you are refusing Mr. Raymonds?"

"No. just giving you the facts. Tell me the time and I will be there.

"How about tomorrow 9:30 am, here at the station?"

"And Mrs. Sanchez?" I hold my breath

"Just you. We will arrange another time to speak with Mrs. Sanchez."

"Tomorrow. 9:30 sharp. "I hang up before he asks anything else of me. I'm not waiting for the cops to look into that phone call. When I have R.W., look into Mr. Fontain's case, he can also take a peek into mine.

When I get home Maria is cleaning the bathroom, she is singing a Spanish song I don't want to startle her so I knock on the inside of the door, she looks up and gives me a her usual big warm smile. She automatically asks, "you alright Mr. Ray? Do you need something?

"No Maria. I have some good news. The police will not be questioning you any time soon." It was a bit of a white lie. She seemed so distraught at the prospect of speaking with them, I wanted to give her a few peaceful days and nights.

"Oh that is maravilloso!"

"Yes it is maravilloso. Hey, why don't we go out and eat tonight? Let's celebrate!"

"Oh Mr. Ray that is too much."

"I won't take no for an answer. Let me hop in the shower and you go spiffy up and..."

"Spiffy up?"

"Put on something other than your uniform. Something nice."

"Can I get a beer tonight?" She smiles sheepishly

"You can have whatever you like."

It's refreshing when the spray of water hits my face. I feel most of the tension leave my body but couldn't help but think, what seemed a short time ago I could put in 12-hour days routinely and now I start to fade in half that time. I turn off the shower and slide the door open just enough to grab a towel. I immediately step back into the confines of the shower enclosure. Don't like the cold air on my warm skin. I dry my hair first then, work my way down to my feet. I wrap the plush towel around my waist and exit. I head over to my dresser where I keep my casual clothing; sweats, an array of colored T-shirts, some tank tops I've never worn and don't like. Something I never told Viv. I pick out a dark blue Polo shirt and a pair of jeans.

I greet Maria at the bottom of the stairs. She is a maroon lace dress, holding her beige purse close to her chest. I offer my arm, "Shall you go Madame?"

The Italian restaurant isn't too busy tonight, being it's a weekday. I pull out her chair. The waiter tells us about the specials and gives us a wine list. I'm not going to drink, especially with the polygraph test tomorrow morning. Maria sees I'm not partaking in alcohol and orders a Coke.

"Maria a lot has happened and I want to know how you are dealing with it all?"

"I don't... What's the word...habitar...dwell on it. I try and keep busy. As you know idle hands are the devil's playthings."

"Are you calling me a devil?"

"Mr. Ray did you bring me to nice place to let me go?"

"Oh for heaven's sake no, I just thought you might start to feel uncomfortable in the house with all that's gone on/"

"Oh... Mr. Ray, I would never leave you. You have had such a hard time." She puts her hands on top of mine. "I know Mrs. Raymonds was not an easy woman to love or easy to take care of. I think Mrs. Raymonds was very sad and very lonely. She don't know what to do with herself. She would try on so many clothes trying to look nice. But can't look nice if your heart filled with anger."

"Yes I think that was true but she wasn't always like that. Remember how she made you laugh and brought you home little gifts for no reason at all? We need to focus on the happy times, not the dark and gloomy ones. I'm trying to hold on to the nice memories, even though it's very hard not to think of the hurt she brought me."

"Si, but when she drank, it get worse. I didn't like her like that. And then she would have many gentl..." Maria stops talking. I pull my hand away and start to rethink my no alcohol policy. "That hurt me inside for you. You understand Mr. Ray?"

"Yes, I understand completely, you worried about me."

"Mrs. Raymonds try and be happy. Dancing around with her loud music, but then she would sit at her desk and be how you say? Color? Blue. I would see her right these long letters and then she would get so mad and rip them up and throw them. When I try pick them up, she yell at me to leave them alone, she would take care of them."

"Letters? What letters? I never saw Viv write any letters. She did all corresponding by emails. My God could they have been attempts at a suicide note?"

"Mr. Ray you were always so busy trying to change the way things were, trying to fix her. I thought whatever she was writing was between her and God. No good come from seeing those letters."

"Do you think she kept any of them?"

"I don't think she ever finished one. I always saw her either balling them up or tearing them apart, most of her personal stuff was locked in the big desk... except for maybe a few little notes she kept in her bedside table."

The waiter arrives with our food. "This look so good." Maria savories every bite. I can barely think of eating. I just want to get home and look through Viv's things. Was what Maria just told me, good news or bad?

When we get home I kiss Maria on the forehead and thank her for a lovely evening.

"Mr. Ray you truly are a good man. Thank you for tonight. Buenas Noches."

I run up to Viv's bedroom. It still smells like her perfume. I pull out the drawer of her little night stand. I find nothing of any consequences, hair appointments reminders. Facials, manicures and spa day appointments (Viv didn't believe in day planner) but nothing that gives me any useful information on the letters she wrote. I'm ready to give up, when I come upon a small piece of paper with a name I know: Jim H, Seaside Motel 10 p.m. My heart drops to my stomach. I knew Viv had admirers, I didn't know that my business partner, the man I knew since law school, was one of them. How could I be so blind so stupid?

I go to the kitchen and make a very strong drink. Polygraph test be damned. I take it to the Rec. Room and sit down in my Lazy Boy chair. I down the drink and stare at our beautiful wedding photo hanging on the wall, this was the place Viv took her final breath. I feel my eyes fill with tears and the sensation of them sliding down my cheeks. The emotional pain is too much and in a fit of rage, without thinking I throw my glass at the wall, just missing the wedding photo.

Maria comes running into the room in her robe and slippers, "Mr. Ray are you alright?"

She sees me bending down, picking up the shards of glass. "Go back to bed Maria! I've got it."

She leaves, only to return with broom and a dust pan. "Mr. Ray, I worry about you. I hope that you..."

I'm not listening to her. I just stare at the mesmerizing fish tank. And thin the fish don't have any idea of emotions; cheerful, mournful, anger. I wonder how I would handle it, if my suspicions were true."

"You go to bed. I will clean up." Maria commands.

"Thank you. I'm sorry."

I drag myself up the stairs to my bedroom. I sit on the bed. My mind is spinning along with the room. I use my feet to remove my shoes, as the second shoe hits the floor, I fall backwards on the bed. I stared at the ceiling. Jim wouldn't betray me, I grab a pillow and crunch it up under my head. I drift off to sleep.

"I would like to make a toast!" Jim raises his glass. "To the two closest friends I have ever had. This is to Bogie and Bacall"

Everyone in the room laughs. Vivian offers her own toast, "We might be Bogie and Bacall, but you and Bob are Bogie and...And-what's his name?"

I answer without delay, "Claude Rains. Claude Rains played Captain Renault in Casablanca."

"I think only three old farts like us would know what we are talking about," Jim says.

"Speak for yourselves gentlemen. I'm still a fine young dame."

"My apologies. I don't know what I was thinking. Ms. Ingrid Bergman ain't got nothing on you." Jim mimics a bow in Viv's direction.

We were so giddy celebrating the new high profile client, Randy Lockford. Jim and I were counting all the prospective money and business he was going to bring to Haverty, Raymonds & Associates. The wine makes Jim very talkative, "Viv I don't know how you put up with this guy?" He sways a bit as he tries to put his arm around my shoulders.

Viv gives me a big grin and a quick peck on the cheek. "He has some redeeming qualities, I must say."

"If you ever get tired of him for not putting the toilet seat down, I would LOVE a roommate. It gets awful lonely at my house." Viv gives Jim a quick peck than stands up and leaves the table. I look to see where she is going but I lose sight of her.

I get up and search the room. I catch a glimpse of her back. She is talking to someone, I can't make out whom. I see her give them a hug and a quick kiss. When she steps away, I see it is Det. Andrews. She is kissing another man now, it is Det. White. I try to go to her but Dr. Radcliff is blocking me, "Bob, you must know that Vivian and I are in love and we..."

"WHAT?! What the hell is going on?"

I jolt awake, breathing heavy from the harrowing nightmare. I know Dr. Radcliff would tell me the stress of finding that note from Jim and the polygraph test today is causing ghastly nightmares, but SHIT! I see my pillow and blankets on the floor. I look at the clock on the night stand, but can't seem to focus. My mouth is as dry as the Mojave Desert or any desert for that matter. I gently swing one leg out, than the other. I scan my room for my slippers but no luck. I slowly stand up from the bed and shuffle to the bathroom.

The bathroom is uncommonly cold. I lean into the shower and turn the nob all the way to hot. The room fills with steam. I gently sit down on the toilet, in my own makeshift steam room and in a low, raspy voice whisper a prayer. "God, please give me peace and calm in my upcoming day."

I hear Maria open my bedroom curtains. She softly knocks on the door, "You sleep okay Mr. Ray?" She must wonder why my bed looks like I wrestled with it and lost. She doesn't bring up my outburst with the glass last night.

"I'm fine. Just need a moment. I will be down shortly. I have to leave early today. So, maybe just some toast and coffee."

On the kitchen table Maria has set out an assortments of cantaloupe, honey dew melons and toast with butter and jam. She pours me a cup of coffee. I don't have the heart to tell her I'm really not hungry, so I force myself to eat one slice of toast and smile.

"This all looks great Maria, but I have an early meeting. So I have to eat and run." I wipe my mouth with a linen napkin she has set out under the silverware when I notice some jelly on my sleeve. "Of course, never fails when you're in a hurry."

"You go change and I will take the shirt to the cleaners."

"Thanks." As I run upstairs to change I remember the call from the cleaners. "Oh and you might want to pick up that jacket while you're there. They said they couldn't get the stain out but are going to give us some coupon."

I pull into the lower-level police station garage. I put up my handicap placard and park right next to the elevator. I hop in and push the button for level 2. When the doors open I follow the arrow, scanning the doors on both sides of the corridor until I find the door with the block letters alerting all to Robbery & Homicide Department.

I walk right in and young male officer, not an Angie Dickinson look-alike, stands up from his desk and greets my like a bartender anxiously waiting for a drink order. "May I help you?"

"My name is Robert Raymonds, I have an appointment with Detective Andrews and Detective White."

"Please have a seat and I will tell them you are here." He motions to the direction of the infamous barbershop chairs.

Before I can even sit down I hear, "Mr. Raymonds thank you for coming in." Det. Andrews says.

I accompany Det. Andrews through a cavalcade of cubicles ranging in size of a small closet to very large spacious living rooms; I can't help but think of a hedge maze. We turn down another hallway where the cubicles disappear and a row of bright, polished brass door knobs seem to pulsate from the fluorescent lights above. As we walk down the hallway I have the strange sensation of walking through a time tunnel. We stop at a door marked occupied. Det. Andrews turns the doorknob and pushes the door open.

The room is small. There is a table with a polygraph machine on it directly behind the table, the wall has a very large generic black electric clock with the cord running down. Opposite the clock is an oversized wall calendar. The whole room has the feeling of an old 1940's film Noir. I have to look at the calendar to remind myself what year it is.

"Please take a seat Mr. Raymonds, Det. Andrews points to a metal chair by the table.

As I sit and can't help but say, "I love what you've done with the place."

"Mr. Raymonds please take a seat, so we can begin. Det. White has been called away."

Sitting on the other side of the table is a bald man in his 60s wearing a cheap grey suit. He has bags under his eyes and a five-day growth on his chin, he has the look of retired employee, supplementing his income giving these tests. I'm also guessing he must have just eaten an onion bagel because as he wires me up I turn my head away from his foul breath.

He instructs me in a monotone voice, "I will ask a few basic questions to start. Do you understand?"

I nod. "You will need to verbally answer. State your name please."

"Robert Raymonds." My hands start to itch.

"Are you currently employed?"

"Yes."

"Is the suit I'm wearing blue?"

"No." Maybe this won't be so bad.

"Did you kill your wife, Vivian Raymonds?" He doesn't look up from the readings on the paper he marks with a pen.

"NO".

"Did you have anything to do with your wife's death?"

"No."

"Do you know who killed your wife?" I pause to think. Suspicions, theories but no evidence.

"Would you like me to repeat the question?" He looks at me directly.

My mind races, trying to analyze what I did and didn't know about Viv.

"Do you know who killed your wife?"

"No."

"Do you know anyone who would want to harm your wife?"

That was a tough one to answer. There was a wide spectrum of people who might want to."

"No."

"Had Vivian Raymonds ever talked about harming herself?"

"I don't know."

"Yes or no answers Mr. Raymonds."

"I don't know the answer. Can anyone really know another person?" The polygrapher looks past me to Detective Andrews who is leaning against the wall. Andrews gives a nod.

"Do you know of a hidden room or passage in your house?" The question confounds me. "What?"

"Do you know of any hidden passages or secret rooms located at 1612 Jenkinson Drive?"

"Yes, there's a hidden passageway from the conservatory to the ballroom, everyone knows that!"

"Mr. Raymond, just answer his questions." Det. Andrews is not amused.

"No! There is no hidden passages or secret rooms in my house. What bullshit question is that?"

"Thank you that is all." The polygrapher moves like molasses as he unhooks the wires attached to me. He closes up his testing machine in a silver briefcase and leaves the room.

"Just wait here for a moment?" Det. Andrews instructs

"How long is a moment? I have things I need to do." I wanted out of this room. I still had to have a very candid conversation with Jim Haverty.

After 10 minutes of pacing, both Det. White and Det. Andrews come in."

"Please take a seat Mr. Raymonnds," Andrews pulls out a chair. "We just want to clarify some questions and your responses you had on the polygraph."

"I told you I have nothing to hide." Det. Andrews is looking over what I assume are my test results. "When the question "Do you know anyone who would want to harm your wife? I see here there was a slight… fluctuation. What do you think might have caused that?"

"Maybe smelling the odor emanating off the polygrapher."

"I'm glad you find this all so funny." Det. White is agitated. "If you are not going to help with this investigation, we're going to consider another recourse."

"I don't know. Listen my wife was no saint. I knew it and I'm sure by now, you guys know it. Like, I told you before, why don't you guys look at some of her so called admirers?" I wasn't sure if I wanted to mention Jim just yet.

"We have considered several people."

"And?"

"We would like to eliminate all possibilities that"...

"I didn't do it! I get that. The spouse is first on the list. But there is a long list of other suspects out there. The sooner you start checking off all the guys my wife slept with! The sooner you can close this case and I can bury my wife!" My heart is thumbing so loud I think the Wonder Twins Detectives can hear it. "Can I go now?!"

"Yes, but you know better than most."

"I know. Don't leave town."

I have no patience to wait for the elevator so I take the stairs. Starting out with a brisk jog, I take two steps at a time but soon my breathing becomes labored and my knees wobbly. I slow down, then come to a stop.

At the bottom of the stairs are too uniform police chatting about their weekend. They take one look at me and became concerned "Hey, you ok buddy?"

I answer slowly, "just trying to stay in shape, or should I say trying to get in shape?"

They both laugh at once. I give a quick wave as I continue, but now I have a pounding headache. I hit the unlock button on my key and slide into the driver seat. I suddenly feel confined and claustrophobic and want out of this dark parking garage, NOW! I grip the steering wheel head for the exit and accelerate my car until the tires screech. I pull out into the morning sunlight and gently lift my foot off the gas pedal. I take a deep breath in and hold it, then slowly let it out. My hands are shaking, I pull off to the side of the road and turn off the engine. I rub my fingers through my hair and feel the tremors in my hands subside. I look in the rearview mirror, "Shit I've got to get myself together, what in the world possessed me to try and run down 2 flights of stairs? I know. Being accused of killing your unfaithful wife and having to confront your best friend and business partner. After taking several breaths I could feel my heart rate beginning to slow down. I jump as my cell phone buzzes. "My God! I'm on edge.

I quickly answer, "Hello... Bob? This is Dr. Radcliffe."

"What's up doc?"

"Gee, I haven't heard that one before. Did I catch you at a bad time? You sound out of breath."

Bad time? That was almost funny.

"Listen, I'm sorry to do this to you now, because of what you're going through, but I have to leave town for a couple of weeks, a family emergency."

"Doc, this REALLY couldn't come at a worse time."" I feel my stomach turn and the headache is now throbbing behind my eyes,

"I'm sorry Bob. I hope you understand?"

"Don't think I have much choice. I hope everything is ok."

"Thank you. Listen, if you have a dire emergency you can always get me through my exchange, but let's hope nothing that drastic would cause you to need to do that."

"I can't promise. I feel I'm not hitting on all cylinders, that feeling like I don't know if I'm coming or going, but I guess it's like Dean says, 'Ain't That A Kick In The Head'. Goodbye Doc."

When I come in the office through the backdoor I see Michelle turning the 'Be Back at 1pm' sign over and locking the door,

"Oh Mr. Raymonds. You startled me.

"Sorry about that. Is Mr. Haverty in?"

"No he is in court today. Would you like me to stay? Do you need anything?"

"No, go to lunch. Leave the front door locked. I have some work I need to finish. I turn to walk away but first ask, "Any messages for me?"

"Yes, there were three. One from Mr. Fontain, one from a R. Wilson and one from, she pauses. Ferndale Funeral Home. I left them on your desk."

"Ok. Thank you."

I watch Michelle leave, then I go straight for Jim's desk. I need to find more proof than a slip of paper that Viv and Jim were sleeping together. I could barely handle the thought of Viv 'hooking' up with strangers. But to think that she and Jim were laughing behind my back was too much.

First place I look is his desk. Nothing in any of the drawers. Then I look through the Law Books, maybe he hid something between the pages. Finally I try the metal cabinet, but it proves to be an obstacle. Every drawer is locked except the top one that is useless, holding only the Yellow Pages, some warranty papers for his car and kitchen appliances. My attention is broken when I hear Jim ask, "Can I help you with something?"

"Yes, you can tell me if you and my wife were sleeping together?!"

"Bob what the hell are you talking about? Is this a joke?"

I show him the small piece of paper with Jim H, Seaside Motel. "I found this in Viv's night stand. Want to tell me what the hell this means?"

"Bob, it's not what you think. I never got the chance to tell you."

"Tell me what? I'm listening now."

"The whole thing started back with the Randy Lockford case. Do you remember? You became obsessed. It took over your life. You would stay up for hours reading and re-reading case files. Then came the uppers to help you focus. You hounded one witness so much, they got a restraining order against you. A restraining order!"

"Ok! I got it. I had some issues. But what does that have to do with you and Viv?"

"I'll tell you. Do you remember sending Viv over to Lockford's late one night?"

"Yeah, we were under a time crunch and we needed his signature. The messenger service was closed and she offered.

Said she wanted to meet him. I regretted that decision every day. I know what happened?"

"You don't know shit, Bob!" Jim says with anger. "You paid no attention to Vivian for months, so someone else did."

"So you are saying this is my fault?!"

"I'm saying she thought your job, the power, the prestige... Meant more to you than her. Vivian was a beautiful, thoughtful, funny woman who wanted her husband to notice her, to love her."

"We were trying to make a name for ourselves, Put our firm on the map. I loved her. I was working those long hours to give her everything she could ever want. She couldn't understand that?"

"What she understood was you were never home. And when you did come home, you were constantly working."

"She didn't have any trouble spending the money my hard work was providing."

"She once told me that shopping was a way to spend her lonely days." His voice begins to tremble, "and the men helped with the lonely nights. Bob you have to understand she wanted to be noticed by you. And if you weren't going to, than damn sure she would find others to. I honestly think she hoped it would make you jealous and you would come around and appreciate her. It was all an act."

"That's bullshit Jim! Maria was here. She saw the men that came and went. That was no act."

"Bob I know what she did hurt you. It hurt her too. In the beginning it was to get your attention, but then I think she started to like the game of it. The money spent on her, the attention. She got caught up in it and then it turned sour...ugly. She told me the night she went to see Lockford, things got way out of hand.

"What do you mean? Way out of hand. What the hell happened?"

"She refused to give me details. All I know that night, she called me crying, saying it would be better for everyone if she wasn't here."

"And you didn't think to tell me? Her husband?"

"We arranged to meet the next morning. She said she was going to check into Seaside Motel and re- evaluate her life. But she called at the crack of dawn the next day and said she was fine. I thought it was best she wasn't alone at a motel. She promised she would talk to you."

"Well she didn't! Apparently she withdrew even more from me. Especially after Lockford accused her of stealing his precious sports memorabilia." Jim and I are too engrossed in our discussion, neither of us hear Michelle buzz us over the intercom.

She makes her way to my desk and quietly says, "Excuse me Mr. Raymonds. Mr. Fountain is waiting to see you."

"Thank you Michelle. Give us five minutes. Then you can send him back."

Jim face is dejected, "Bob I can't tell you how sorry I am. But I swear nothing happened between us. You have to believe me!"

"I don't know what to believe right now Jim. I'm just hanging on by a thread. I just want this whole thing to be over. I want to find out who and what killed my Viv. That's all I know right now." Jim and I both know we are at a stale mate. Before we can say anything else, Mr. Fontain is walking towards my desk.

He greets us with a huge smile. "I can't thank you enough Mr. Raymonds. You and Mr. Haverty have saved my life." Once her scumbag lawyer, oh sorry. Once her lawyer got the evidence that you sent, they totally buckled."

"Once we were able to obtain the phone records and interview some of your wife's acquaintances and several of her boyfriend's colleagues- their whole plan fell apart. I don't think their relationship will stand the test of time. In fact, they both offered dirt on each other."

"Those two deserve each other". He reaches into his jacket pocket and hands us a check. "This should cover everything. I can't thank you guys enough. If you ever need anything."

"Thank you Mr. Fontain we appreciate your business." Jim says. "If you could wait out in the lobby, we have some papers we need you to sign." He thanks us again and walks back to Michelle's desk.

"That was fast Bob. How did you accomplish all that in such a short time?"

I show him one of the messages left on my desk. Regarding A. Fontain issue. Sent all relevant items to her lawyer. Hope it helps. R.W.

"It seems that our 'friend' R.W. Comes through again."

"You know I wasn't too sure about him when you handed to use his services Bob. But he does come in handy. Let's count this as a win."

I look at the check and shake my head. "$1,000 doesn't seem like a win."

"What do you expect? It's never going to be like it was. Those days are over. Listen we really need do discuss this issue about Viv further. You have the wrong idea."

"I can't do this now Jim." He walks out of the office without saying anything.

He is right. Those days are over. It can never be like it was. I leave out the back door. I don't want to see anyone.

I turn the engine off and head for the house knowing the front door is very seldom locked. I walk in and with a medium loud voice I call out, "anyone home, Maria?" A bit louder, "Maria?" There is no response, the house is quiet.

I walk towards her room in the back of the house. I knock on her door and call out her name. The room is as I imagined, spotless, bed neatly made, the items on her vanity organized. A lace doily on an end table by her bed that holds a small lamp, the Good Book (The Bible) with rosary beads resting on the top. Her private bathroom door is open, I take a quick glance and see nothing out of the ordinary. I try not to panic as I run around the house calling out her name. My pace picks up as I run upstairs, I stop and look out the large pane window midway up the staircase; there she is, outside on her hands and knees between the cobblestone pathway on the side of the house. I tap on the window to get her attention. She stands up slowly and smiles as she looks up toward me. I motion her in.

"I'm so sorry Mr. Ray. I didn't hear you come home." She removes her large brim hat and washes her hands.

"Maria, you scared the you-know-what out of me."

"It was such a nice day I thought I would get outside and get some fresh air and sun. Can I fix you something to eat?"

"No thanks. You know Maria you don't have to pull weeds, we have someone that does that."

"No, I didn't do that. I saw something glisten by the pathway. I go to look."

"And what was it? Buried treasure?"

"I find nothing. Must be some reflection from a window or the wind chimes."

"So no buried treasure? Darn! You know I started to worry when you didn't answer. My mind went to the dark side there for a second."

"Sorry I worry you Mr. Ray. I go start dinner and bring your drink to you. You look so tired."

"It's been a very long day."

I head to the Rec. Room and see that the red light is flashing on my desk telephone answering machine. That's strange because Maria usually answers the phone. I hit the button and listen to the message. The only thing I hear is a dial tone, Must be a wrong number or one of those robo calls. The answering machine states the call was received by 1:20.

"Mr. Ray I brought your drink and some cheese and crackers." She pauses as she steps through the doorway. "I'm sorry are you busy?"

"No, there was a call that came in today, but no message was left, just a dial tone."

"I did not hear the phone ring. Maybe I was outside."

"Here let me have that famous Vodka and Tonic of yours." I take the drink off the tray along with a small plate of cheese and crackers, with a steady hand I make my way back to the desk. Balancing the drink and the plate of cheese and crackers, never spilling a drop. Something I learned from my father. I set them down on the desk and plant my butt in the desk chair. I take a long drink and my whole-body flows with a warm sensation. I look over at the fish tank, "if you guys could only talk. You were all here that fateful afternoon."

I look out the French doors at the calm early evening. I decide I also could use some fresh air. I turn the bronze handles of the double doors and try and push them both open but they don't budge. I realize the deadbolt was set securely near the top of the door. I reach up and wiggle it free. I make my way out to the small patio and take a seat on the bench, not afraid to spill any of my drink, it was half gone. I can see why Maria took a little break here. The weather is perfect, I feel the warmth of the sun against my face. I look over at the pathway in between the cobblestones; small blades of grass and weeds were sneaking out between the stones. Ok she was not pulling weeds. My glass is empty and I could use some more cheese for my left over cracker. As I head back inside I look down and notice a strange substance sprinkled around both French doors. At first, I think it's just bird poop, but as I get closer I realize it's not. I bend down onto one knee to investigate, when suddenly and without warning my back tightens up like I was in a huge vice and it was being tightened up with every move I make. I freeze in the bending position, afraid to move in any direction. I stay there in a "Tim Tebow" position trying to relax my back muscles which is impossible. I should know better to even try. I use the French door handle for leverage and try to hoist myself up into a standing position. I make it, and very slowly try walking half bent over and back into the room. I reach the desk and pull open one of the drawers and retrieve a small piece of paper from a note pad. I very gingerly make my way back to the area where the unknown substance lays.

I let out a slight groan as I bend down and scoop up the white substance onto the paper with the help of my shoe.

I yell loudly for Maria, she comes running. "What is it Mr. Ray?" She sees I'm hunched over like Quasimodo and runs to help me stand up straight.

"Go to the kitchen and get me a Ziploc bag!" She must have thought the bag was going to help my back. She was confused by the request.

"I don't understand Mr. Ray. What do you want?

"Please Maria! A Ziploc bag, just do it."

With a gentle tiny stride, she quickly leaves. When she returns, she helps me walk over to the desk. "Please go upstairs and get my pain pills, you know where I keep them." As Maria hurries upstairs, I place the paper with the unknown substance into the Ziploc bag, seal it and place it in the desk drawer. I had no idea what it is but my gut feeling told me it needed to be analyzed.

Maria comes back with two pills and a glass of water. "Here you go Mr. Ray."

"Thank you." I swallow the pills. "Maria I'm going to go soak in a hot bath that usually helps my back untighten."

"Do you need help up the stairs Mr. Ray?"

"No, I got it. I will just take it slow and use the handrail and wait for the pills to kick in." I lied. After taking just one step I knew I needed the help she offered. It seems to take us forever to reach the top. I go straight for the tub and turned on the water, as hot as I think my body can take. I slowly sit down on the toilet and bring my right leg up to untie my shoe. I notice a small white stain on my slacks around the knee area. It looks like the same substance on my coat jacket. "What the hell is this stuff? I take off my slacks and let them fall to floor. I'm in no shape to fold them. Steam is filling the room. I cautiously step into the tub. As the hot water, Vodka Tonic and pains pills relax my muscles, my mind struggles to figure out what the strange white substance could be. When the tub water starts to cool I know it's time to get out.

I try to lift my body out of the tub, but my arms are wet noodles, I have no strength. I try to yell for Maria, but only a whisper comes out. What is happening to me? Suddenly, it all goes black.

When I open my eyes I'm surrounded by people, none of which I recognize. I turn my head from side-to-side to see where the hell I am. Thank God! In my own bathroom.

"Mr. Raymonds can you hear me?"

I don't know who was saying it, but I do recognize Maria's frantic voice, "is he going to be alright?"

A young man inches from my face is asking me questions, "Mr. Raymonds, do you know where you are?"

My voice is dry, but I get out one word, "home."

"Do you think you can sit up?" He helps sit me up.

"What happened?" I whisper

"That's what we are trying to figure out. Did you slip coming out of the tub?"

I now realize not only am I lying on the cold floor of my bathroom with several strangers surrounding me but I'm naked except for a small wash cloth covering my private parts. "All I can tell you is everything went black."

"So you did not fall and hit anything?"

"I don't think so. I really don't remember. Can someone hand me a robe?" Maria burst through the mass of firemen and EMT and hands me my robe.

"Dear Jesus! I heard loud thump and you don't answer me." She makes the sign of the cross."

"Mr. Raymonds, I think it's best we take you to the hospital. Your vitals are a bit low and we don't know what caused the blackout. You should be monitored overnight."

"Please Mr. Ray. Go to hospital. I will come with you." I agree.

A little scared of what is happening to me, I lay down on the gurney and let the EMT do their job. I'm loaded into the ambulance. Most of my neighbors are milling around talking with each other. I can't make out any words only mumbling.

That is until I hear the unmistakable voice of my good neighbor Larry. "Gee, Bob, what's going on now?!"

Larry seems more concerned about the reputation of the neighborhood than my health. "Jesus, this place is a magnet for trouble. First the murder and now this."

The EMT slides me into the back of the ambulance. I don't have the energy to say anything. "I follow you Mr. Ray. I be right behind you, you will see, everything will be good."

We reach the hospital in minutes. I'm not in critical condition, so no sirens. My gurney is pushed down the hallway, where I hear voices from all directions. I feel the sudden gust of air as two large doors open automatically. A young woman with short cropped hair and bright pink lipstick greets me. "We're going to have you slide over onto this bed" she hands me a hospital gown. "And have you change into this. Do you need any help?"

"No, I got it." She pulls the curtain closed as I change. After getting into my gown, I just lay back and close my eyes and wait.

"Mr. Raymonds." A doctor pulls open the curtain. Somewhere in his late sixties, may be even older, he has pure white hair, clean shaven and holding a medical chart. He gets right to the point, no small talk "Your vitals are a bit better now," he doesn't look up from the chart. "It's really just more of a precaution."

"And you would be?"

"Oh, I'm sorry. I'm Dr. Grayson. I'm the attending physician on duty tonight and like I was saying, everything looks good we are just going to keep you overnight and wait and see. Right now we are waiting for a room to open up."

"So, I can go home tomorrow?"

"If everything checks out, I don't see why not. I will have a nurse come in and check on you." And with that he disappears like The Wizard of Oz behind the curtain. The young nurse with the bright pink lipstick comes in and hands me a tiny paper cup with two pills in them, "this will help you sleep." I don't want to tell her I had taken two pain pills earlier. All I really wanted to do was sleep. I throw them in my mouth and that's the last thing I remember. They worked faster on me than ether did, when I had my tonsils out as a young boy.

When I open my eyes, I see the bright sun shining through my windows. I push the remote-control for my bed to lift the back. I lean over to pour water into a plastic cup. I refill it two or three times until my thirst has subsides a bit.

"Nice to see you. How are you doing?" Standing in the doorway is Det. Andrews and Det. White. I don't know which one asked the question. "How are you feeling?" Det. Andrews.

"I've been better. I've been worse." I take another a sip of water. The detectives step into the room.

"How did you know I was here?"

"We stopped by your house and we were informed by your neighbor before we even reached the front steps."

"Oh yeah, that must have been Larry. He's such a wonderful guy." I say sarcastically. I take another sip of water. Waiting to see why the two detectives have come by

"Mr. Hamilton, that is Larry's last name, is it not? Had some choice words for you Mr. Raymonds."

"Oh do tell, what did that prick have to say now?"

"He thought maybe you had tried to commit suicide over the guilt of killing your wife."

"What the fu..?" I sit straight up. I'm angry and I want both of them to know it. "So, you guys here to arrest me?"

"So, you're telling us there is some truth to what Mr. Hamilton is alleging?" Det. White asks.

"NO! … No God damn it!"

Det. White continues with the questions. "Well he tells us there were some pretty nasty arguments over at your house, and other neighbors would verify it."

"Jesus Christ, it is in all the police reports that were taken when they were called. But being the fine detectives you are, you already know that." I don't know what else you want from me? I have been honest with you guys about Vivian's past indiscretions. I have cooperated by taking a lie detector test... I have nothing to hide. Talk to my neighbors! Talk to my friends! Talk to my colleagues, but get this straight. Don't talk to me. I'm through answering anymore of your questions.""

Detective Andrews moves to the bed. "We just want to find out what happened. The sooner you realize we are not your enemy, the faster this will all be behind you. Good day Mr. Raymonds."

As I watch them leave I simultaneously push the nurse's button. A few seconds later a large African American woman comes in and gruffly asks, "What do you want?"

"I NEED to go home! As much as I like my good night's sleep, I would rather be out of this hospital and this gown. I tug at the chest to make my point. Please I just want to go home."

"It's not up to me Mr. Raymonds. I will page your doctor and have him come talk to you."

As she leaves the room, I say out loud, "Great bed side manner there."

I have no clothes when I came in, so I head out the door with the hospital gown wrapped around me and my right hand holding the back closed. I make a beeline to the bank of elevators a short distance down the corridor. Before I can push the red arrow button, I hear a stern voice cry out.

"Where do you think you are going Mr. Raymonds?!"

I instantly feel my blood pressure rise and my heart rate accelerate. I make a slow, deliberate turn, my jaw tightens and my eyes squint with rage. It is the same nurse I discussed going home with. She has one arm propped on the counter of the nurse's station; like a gunslinger leaning against the bar of a saloon, waiting for a confrontation. I'm in no mood for a standoff. "I'm going home and I don't have to answer to you."

Her eyes widen and she stands up straight up, "Mr. Raymonds, I told you I would call your doctor. I am sorry if you don't like that." I don't believe she has ever been sorry.

Our duel continues, I don't move away from the elevator. So she changes tactics. In an apologetic tone, one I bet she seldom uses, "Why don't you go back to your room and I will page Dr. Grayson again."

"Call him or Doc Brown or Doctor Zhivago. Anyone you can to release me!" I can see by the expressions of the other nurses in the surrounding area they are amused with the verbal beat down she was enduring. I reluctantly go back to my room

I dial out on the hospital phone and call Maria at the house, it goes straight to voicemail. I think of calling Jim, but I'm not ready to see him. I'm desperate enough to call Mike or Hank, one of my poker buddies but my prayers are answered. Walking in the room is my angel, Maria.

"You are a sight for sore eyes, Maria."

"I come at visiting hours Mr. Ray. How are you feeling?"

"I will feel a lot better once I get home."

"You go home today?"

"Yes, I will go home today."

I send Maria home to get me some clothes while I speak with the on call doctor, promising him I would make a follow appointment with my general practitioner. Then I signed my legal rights away from suing anyone who has ever worked or visited this hospital. And finally after two hours, I am released AMA

An elderly white-haired man, standing no more than 5 ft. tall comes in the room pushing a wheelchair.

"I don't need that, thank you."

He cups his hand around his ear, "What?"

"I don't need the wheelchair, sir. See I can walk perfectly fine." I demonstrate by walking around in a circle."

"Sorry son, hospital policy. Plus I would like to keep this job." He jokes. He is more than likely a volunteer. I don't want to be a dick to this man who probably served his country. I get in the wheelchair.

The elderly gentleman waits with me in the lobby. I see outdated magazines on the table with all the address labels torn off. Sports Illustrated, Good Housekeeping, and Reader's Digest. I notice an article on AARP, 'How to Save for the

End'. Right there is dawns on me, I have done nothing for Viv's funeral. We never really talked about it. What should I arrange for her service?

I see Maria headed in my direction carrying a small overnight case. I tell the elderly gentleman, "I need to go to the men's room to change into my clothes please."

He wheels me over the bathroom and releases the wheelchair brake. "I will wait out here, unless you think you need help young man."

"I'll be fine, thank you." I give him a quick military salute and he returns it with a smile.

When we get home Maria helps me upstairs to bed. She fluffs my pillows, tucks in the sheets and straightens the bed spread. She flutters around me in a state of dismay.

"Mr. Ray, do you need anything?"

"Maria, I'm fine. Just go about your business. I didn't have brain surgery. Really, I'm ok."

"You call me if you need anything, comprende?"

"I do need one thing, can you bring me my phone."

"Mr. Ray I don't think it is good idea you work."

"I'm not going to work. I need to call the funeral home."

"Of course."

I call the funeral home that I used for my mom. A pleasant woman's voice answers, "Ferndale Funeral Home, how may I help you?"

"Yes, hello. My name is Robert Raymonds and I would like to know if my wife Vivian Raymonds has been...has been delivered to you yet."

"I'm sorry for your loss. Can you hold one moment please?"

"Sure." She puts me on hold and I hear the soft sounds of elevator music's rendition of The Rose.

The lovely voice comes back on the line. "I'm sorry Mr. Raymonds, your wife is not here. The police have not released her body yet."

"What do you mean?" I feel throbbing in my head. My face turning hot.

"Mr. Raymonds I can connect you with our director. He can answer your questions."

"No, I know who will me answering my questions. Thank you." I hang up and instantly dial the Wonder Twins. It goes straight to voicemail. I leave an angry tirade of expletives.

Maria hears my profanity shouting and rushes upstairs, "Mr. Ray what is it?"

The emotional flood gates open and tears poured out. "Oh God! Oh God, she is laying there on that cold slab in that dark locker. I loved her. I never stopped." Maria says nothing. She walks over and pats my forearm. "I understand you sorrow, Mr. Ray"

I sleep through the sunrise and into the late morning. The sound of the house phone ringing wakes me up. I wait to see if Maria will pick up, after five rings the message matching kicks on. I can make out a man's voice leaving the message but not what he was saying.

I try calling Dr. Radcliff's emergency number on my cell, but it goes straight to voicemail, "You have reached the emergency number of Dr. Radcliff. Please leave your number and me or my associate Dr. Straub will call you back. Thank you. BEEP.

"Doc Radcliff, this is Bob Raymonds. Can you please call me back! Things are falling apart and I really NEED to talk to you! Cell is 555-2239 or home 555-7816. But I'm sure you have those numbers." BEEP.

I look at the clock on the nightstand and it was 20 minutes to noon. I put pants on, no shirt or shoes. I head straight to the answering machine in the Rec. Room. The light is flashing, I push the button and listened to a man's voice.

"Hello Mr. Raymonds. This is Dr. Grayson. I'm checking in on how you are doing. The on call doctor, Dr. Ellis and the nurses said you were quite anxious to leave. I hope you are feeling better and it's nothing the staff did. I hope your two visitors were able to contact you. Please call if you have any questions. The number is 555-1968.

I dial the number right back. I hear the phone start to ring and I'm prepared to leave a voice message. After three rings I hear the voice loud and clear, "Dr. Grayson," I wait for the instructions to leave after the beep. "Hello, this is Doctor Grayson."

I'm stunned he answers, "Oh, I'm sorry doctor I had it in my mind a voice mail would be coming on, that's why the delay. This is Bob Raymonds. I was returning your call, to say thanks for all your help."

"How are you feeling? Any dizzy spells?"

"I feel pretty good."

"Have you made a follow up appointment with your doctor?"

"Not yet- but I will. I promise. I just have a lot on my plate right now. But since I have you on the phone, the visitors you are talking about are the two police detectives, right?"

"No. These two visitors came in after you left?

"Maybe poker buddies checking in on me? My housekeeper might have told them I was in the hospital?

"No, I don't think so. I was making rounds on the floor and I heard one gentleman say he was your neighbor Larry something. The charge nurse Ms. Katie spoke with the other gentleman. He donated his flowers to the nurses. I can connect you to the nurse's station if it's important."

"Yes, thank you."

"Remember call your doctor! Hold for just a minute."

"Nurses station C."

"Yes hello. This is Mr. Raymonds. This might sound strange but I was a patient and I hear that a visitor, a man, left some flowers there for you wonderful Florence Nightingales." I was laying it on thick, but I had to know who else came by. I figured Larry wanted to gloat or raise my blood pressure so high I would stroke out. But who was the other guy.

"Hold on I will see if it's still here." She comes back after a moment. "The card reads, sorry partner."

Of course, Jim would want to see how I was after being rushed to the hospital in an ambulance. You can't erase 20 years in one terrible fight.

"Wait, there is something written on the back of the card. Love Big Jim."

I can't believe it, why is Big Jim in town right now? Did he see the news reports on Viv's death? Was that the reason? I know it's not to see how I was doing. I haven't seen or heard from him in over a year, there must be another reason. His sudden appearance puzzles me so much I start pacing back and forth in front of the aquarium.

Could there be a connection with the appearance of Larry and Big Jim at the hospital on the same day? Could either one of them have anything to do with Viv's death. The one thing I knew for certain, is Viv did not like Big Jim and Larry has a strong dislike for me. The best way to get some of the answers was to meet face-to-face and ask why the sudden interest in my well-being? If the police weren't going to do their due diligence, I would.

I quickly put on shirt and shoes and cut across my shared backyard lawn and right up to Larry Hamilton's back door.

The door is open but the screen door is closed and locked. I know better than to knock on the screen door that would make very little noise, so I knock on the wood molding and call out his name. I can hear him off in the distance yell, "Who is it?"

"It is your next-door neighbor, Bob." I hear him make his way towards the door, only the screen door separating us.

Visibly annoyed by my presence, "Just what do you want?"

"Hey what's with the attitude? Didn't you want to see me? You came to the hospital." He is lost in the shadows of the screen door, I feel uncomfortable talking to the bodiless voice. "Can you come out or ask me in? I find this arrangement very unnerving." Silence.

"Yeah, come in." He holds the door open, I take one step in as he takes two steps back.

"Well, tell me why you came to see me at the hospital."

"No big mystery."

"It is to me! We both know we don't care that much for each other, so why you would be there?"

"I'll tell you why! It's because you don't like me. I was worried you point the finger at me for your wife's death. You would tell lies to the cops or try and frame me anyway possible."

"My God Larry. You and your imagination is running wild. What do you mean lies Larry? We all know you had a thing for my wife."

"Yes, I was extremely attracted to your wife and when I drank, which is almost every day, I got brave and went over to your place. She was outside in her bikini and I, well you know was overcome with..."

"Don't tell me, lust, and desire, covet the whole nine yards of wanting my wife."

"Yes, but nothing happened. First, she was nice and told me I better get back home and have some coffee, but when I moved in a little too close she hit me with a closed fist that knocked me off balance. I felt so ashamed, I turned and went home. We never said another word about it."

"Well Larry, I am glad you told me this story, but you see Viv told me the whole story when I got home that night. I was headed over to your place as soon as I heard this but she calmed me down and told me she took care of it."

"Look Bob, you were gone most of the time and it's not like you guys had the storybook marriage."

"Meaning?" Larry really knew how to push my buttons.

"The fights, the cops being called, the amount of male friends she had. Don't pretend it was some goddam fairytale."

I wasn't about to discuss anything about my marriage to this asshole. "Larry I think for your safety and my sanity we don't say anything to each other. Not hi or goodbye or Merry Christmas. I don't want to ever see your slimy, sleazy face again. Got it?" I turn and walk out. I don't even turn around when he slams his door shut.

I head back to my house, one down and one to go. I cross Larry off my list of potential suspects but down deep I never thought he was ever a serious candidate for any misdeeds involving Viv, he was just a belligerent alcoholic. Now on to Big Jim and what brought him to town. I didn't think I would have any trouble finding him, after his trial he insisted we exchange our information, which included all phone numbers, home, cell, and office.

I go over to my desk and look up Big Jims cell number and dial it. I was on a roll and I didn't want to slow down, couldn't help but think of the expression, "Strike While The Iron Is Hot." I take a deep breath and wait for him to answer. I recognize his burly voice, it's though I talked to him yesterday.

"Hey, how they hangin' Jim?"

"Who the hell is this?"

"That hurts. You mean you don't recognize the voice of the man that kept you out of jail and saved you hundreds of thousands in lawsuits?"

"Well I'll be damned, if it isn't my favorite lawyer of all time. How you doing partner? You know, I went by the hospital to see you?"

"Yes, I heard. How did you know I was in the hospital?"

"You're not going to believe it. I was coming to your house and I saw you being put into the ambulance. I was going to ask that Mexican lady"

"Maria, her name is Maria."

"I was going to ask her but she was a basket case, Next thing I know she is following the ambulance in a car. She is one faithful servant." Big Jim as crass as ever.

"Jim level with me. No bullshit! What do you want?"

"Shit, there ain't no conning you. You probably know me better than anyone. Well first I wanted to see how you were doing. I heard about Viv's passing. So sorry, she was a fine lady. And I mean fine both ways, not just beautiful but classy and smart."

"Thank you. It has all been a shock."

"I bet. Hey, since you are out of the hospital, why don't I come over, bring some brews and we can just shoot the shit?"

"Jim I'm really not up for visitors just yet. I have a lot..."

Jim interrupts. "Listen, there is something else I need to talk to you about." I should I have known. 'Big Jim' Marshall always has ulterior motives. "Did Viv ever talk about a file she was holding for me?"

"What the hell are you talking about Jim? A file? What a tax file?"

"This particular file is very important. So I'm asking if she might have said anything about it?"

"Is this a joke? If it is, it's not funny! My wife is dead. The cops are questioning me and I just got out of the hospital. And you have the gall to ask about some file?!" I'm just about to hang up but Jim turns to pleading.

"This is a personal file that could cause me some embarrassment. I'm begging you could look around for it. Is there a place Viv might have kept important papers? Did she have a safe deposit box? You know I wouldn't ask for such a favor unless it was imperative I get it back in my possession. Please Bob! Do what you can to try and find it."

My God what was in this file that made him so desperate? His desperation pivot to bribing. "I can make it very profitable for you. That I can guarantee." Now I had no doubt Viv knew something about Jim Marshall I did not; the question was what? "I can't stress enough the importance this document is to me."

"Jim, I don't see or hear from you in over a year and now you're calling me about some file you think my deceased wife kept? I don't have time for this!"

"I agree Bob, I know it's a shitty time. Who knows maybe it has been accidently thrown away or been destroyed."

"There might be some boxes in the garage. If I feel up to it, I will take a look around."

"Oh, that would be great. I can't ask for more than that! I can come over and help look. Maybe you shouldn't be doing anything strenuous."

"I will give you a call if I run across it. I've got to go." I don't wait for a reply, I hang up. His voice wears on my nerves.

This whole business with the mystery file was moving Big Jim up the list of suspects. I couldn't help but wonder, just how far would he go to find out if Viv had his folder, or knew where it was. The man had no morals or conscious?

I figured I could eliminate Larry as a suspect. He was a creep for sure, but not a murderer. The next guy who I never really did eliminate was Randy Lockford. I know he has a temper.

He was irate, claiming Viv was responsible for some of his very expensive memorabilia missing. He called and vented his anger with some very descriptive language. He screamed and threaten broken legs with baseball bats and lawsuits. And of course, I believed that was all it was - missing property. But now with the new information Jim Haverity told me, I wasn't so sure. Only Viv and Randy really know what took place that night. And she wouldn't tell me. Maybe he didn't care for her no-nonsense in your face personality or maybe she broke off their affair if they ever had one and he didn't like that. Or what she told Jim was true, she said no and he felt his manhood being challenged and lost his temper? Shit, she got me so upset I had dreams about killing her I knew how she could be, so I am not ready to cross off Mr. Lockford from my list.

I should know better than trying to solve a crime. Through the years working as a lawyer I would get the urge to gather clues, solve the crime, to play Perry Mason. On numerous occasions Jim would say, "That is not our job Bob." Was I in over my head?

The doorbell rings. "Maria? Could you get the door?" Than it rings again. "Maria?' She doesn't answer. As I walk to the door, there is a hard knock. "I'm coming".

I open the door and standing there are Detectives Andrews and White. I greet them with a simple hello.

"Good afternoon Mr. Raymonds, may we come in?"

"Sure." I step aside as they proceed in. "I was going to call you."

"We got your other messages." Repsons Det. White

"What message?"

"About your wife. And how we never released Mrs. Raymonds body to the funeral home and how we were low lifes and inconsiderate assholes.

"Look, I'm sorry. But you have to understand, I would like to lay my wife to rest."

"And you have to understand Mr. Raymonds- this is a homicide investigation."

"I know. And that's why I was going to call you. I have some potential suspects."

Det. White isn't subtle with is thoughts. "Jesus H. Christ. You are lawyer. We are the detectives! Let us do our job."

I ignore Det. White and turn to Det. Andrews, "I have talked with a few people that have had contact with my wife within a few weeks prior to her death."

"Yes, we received a phone call from your neighbor, Larry Hamilton. He said you were harassing him." Det. Andrews tells me.

"That's bullshit. If there was any harassing going on it was from him to my wife. It doesn't matter. I took him off my list of suspects."

"A list?! You have a suspect list? Tell me Mr. Raymonds. Did you put yourself on this suspect list?" Det. White chuckles. "Do you believe this, Nick?"

I have the urge to punch Det. White in the mouth, but I continue. "There's Randy Lockford, he was quite upset with several memorabilia items that came up missing, a short time after I sent Viv to his house to sign some documents. He called and said expensive items were gone and they came up missing shortly after she was in his apartment. And let me tell you he threw out four letter words I haven't even heard of. He definitely has some anger issue."

"Mr. Raymonds, I believe you underestimate our ability to investigate. We spoke to Mr. Lockford about the missing items. That issue has been resolved. The missing items have been tracked down." Det. Andrews says.

"Hey Columbo, I bet you didn't know that it was Lockford who called the day your wife died?" Det. White is goading me.

"Are you sure?"

"Yes." He told us he called to apologize to your wife for the accusation of the theft."

"I told him she didn't do it."

"He said all of it had been a huge misunderstanding."

"Was it a big misunderstanding when he came on to her? You would think that after getting him off from doing prison time and losing millions in salary and endorsement deals. He would have the balls to call me, himself. I hope the asshole bats under 200 and gets cut!"

I hear Maria come in through the kitchen back door, "Mr. Ray I see a car out front. Is it the Wondering Twins?" Maria is embarrassed when she sees the detectives and me talking in the living room. "Oh, ser arrepentido. I didn't know you..."

"It's ok Maria." She slightly bows her head and quickly leaves the room."

"Did she mean to say Wonder Twins? From that 70's cartoon show? Det. Andrews asks.

I shrug my shoulders, "Ummm..."

"Det. Andrews and I came by to tell you that the cornor is releasing Mrs. Raymonds body to the funeral home by the end of today." Both detectives head for the door. "Please Mr. Raymonds leave the police work to us and leave your neighbor alone."

I open the door, "I can't promise on either. But I appreciate you coming by to tell me about Viv." I'm just about to shut the door when I ask, "by the way. Where did Mr. Lockford's memorabilia turn up?"

Det. White takes a call on his cell and continues to the car but Det. Andrews stops and turns towards me. "It was found in Las Vegas. It appears that his butler or assistant, Mr. Tan is quite a gambler and evidently not good one. He owes thousands of dollars to various casinos. The insurance investigator tracked down the stolen items. The funny thing is Mr. Tan sold them for half their market value. As guess he wasn't much of a baseball fan. Now I hear, he is trying to sell his story to the tabloids as he serves his time for grand theft. Maybe Mr. Lockford will be losing some of those endorsement deals after people read Mr. Tan's book. Rumor is there's more dirt in that book than a slide for home plate."

"It couldn't happen to a nicer guy. That high-price prima donna, living in his sheltered world, expecting everything handed to him because he can hit and catch a ball."

"Remember Mr. Raymonds, leave the investigating to the professionals." He joins Det. White who has started the car.

So, I didn't have all the facts concerning Randy. I won't make that mistake again. Before I tell the Wonder Twins to check out Big Jim Marshall, I'm going see if this folder exists and what the hell is in it.

If it was important enough for Big Jim to come see me, I don't think Viv would have stored it in a box of papers in the garage.

I start with her night stand, the same one I found the note about the motel. I try her dresser. When I open all the drawers the smell of her perfume lingers in the air. My search starts to turn frantic.

Maria comes upstairs and sees I am looking for something. "May I help?"

"I'm looking for a folder Mrs. Ray might have brought home quite a while ago."

"Will it help find who killed Mrs. Ray?

"I don't know. Let's just say some interested parties want it back really bad. It is very important to them."

Than it dawns on me.

When Viv and I were looking for furniture, we were sold on a particular Queen Size bed; the salesman should us a feature neither of us had ever seen, but both thought it was very intriguing. In the back of the head board a hidden compartment almost invisible to the naked eye. I couldn't help but think if there is a file anywhere in this house, it could only be here.

I bend down at the foot of the bed where a small release lever was located. I see the compartment has sprung open maybe a quarter inch. Even knowing what I was looking for, it was almost impossible to see. I pulled the bed away from the wall to make it easier to bend and look into the compartment, the hideaway is deep and I have to reach into the back.

"Oh who would think of something like that? Very clever." I forgot Maria was still in the room.

I reach in grab something and drag it towards me. As soon as it came into the dim bedroom light I could see its manila folder with the Big Jim's company logo printed along the top.

"Mr. Ray is that it?"

I stand up and find the nearest chair. I'm so nervous, my hands begin trembling and are moist with sweat. I pull out the contents of the folder. It doesn't take long for me to see why Big Jim was so anxious to get it back. Instantly my stomach twists and acid is burning a hole in my stomach lining.

"What is it Mr. Ray?"

"Maria can you go downstairs and get me some TUMS and a glass of milk?"

"Is it a bad thing, Mr. Ray?"

"Please Maria. Can you just do it?"

"Si' Mr. Ray."

Inside the folder is a disgusting photo of a man raping young boy, no older than six or seven. I have the urge to vomit not knowing if it's the image or the abundance of acid flowing in my abdomen. I set the folder aside. My mind can't comprehend what it is seeing. The torture of innocent child, I can't look anymore. As I'm leaving the room, Maria is entering with a glass of milk and two pink antacid tablets. I down the milk and the pills. "Sorry, I'm going need something stronger than milk. Can you go make me a double Maria?"

I head downstairs to the Rec. Room and collapse onto my desk's swivel chair. "What in the hell was Viv doing with this?" I pause to look at the fish in the aquarium; smoothly and silently swimming in and out of the beautiful colored coral. A pleasure I usually enjoyed, that brought a relaxing calm over me. But no amount of fish gazing or TUMS or even liquor was going to relax my brain or my insides.

"Mr. Ray, I have your drink." She comes in balancing the drink on a silver stray and a cloth napkin across her forearm. There is no way I want Maria to see the folder contents so I put them in desk drawer and lock it. "I must say you look like a professional waitress and you didn't spill a drop."

She smiles, bends at her waist, "I am here for you. Anything you need you call me."

"Maria I don't know what I would do without you. I'm so thankful for your loyalty." I'm also thankful she doesn't ask to see what is in the folder.

I take one sip of the drink, than set in down on the desk. There is a bad taste in my mouth and a queasy feeling in my gut. The graphic photos have taken a toll on my body and soul.

I go down the hallway. Open kitchen door and lean my head in, "Maria I'm done for tonight. I'm going upstairs to bed."

"Mr. Ray are you sure I can't call doctor for you?" She is wiping her hands on the towel she keeps tucked in her apron. I don't think she realizes she does it all the time. It's like some nervous impulse, like someone who bites their finger nails, an unconscious habit.

"I will be fine with a good night's sleep. Why don't you go out to a movie or visit a friend?" I wasn't sure Maria had any close friends. She had church acquaintances, her sister and the estranged husband

"I couldn't do nothing like that Mr. Ray, I need to be here if you need something during the night, I would feel bad if something happened to you and I was not here. I can always go out other times when you are feeling mucho better."

"Goodnight Maria."

"Good night Mr. Ray I hope you can relax and get your mind off your troubles. I fix you nice breakfast, manana."

I close the bedroom curtains and grab the remote. I want the sickening photos out of my mind. I channel surf until I come across an old episode of "You Bet Your Life" with Groucho Marx.

I undress and get into my pajamas, keeping one eye on the TV. I get in bed, lean up against my propped-up pillows and hope that Groucho can make me forget. My eyes are heavy and I try to stay awake, afraid of what I might dream. The last thing I hear is- "And now here is, the one, the only GROUCHO MAR.

"Mr. Ray did you sleep well?" Maria is opening my curtains, my eyes squint from the morning sun aiming into my room.

I ask, "What time is it?"

She bends down and picks up my slippers. "It is almost 9 a.m."

"My God no wonder you came up here, you must have thought I die..." I don't finish my thought. "Can you make me some oatmeal? I just want something easy today."

"Si, Mr. Ray, I fix you more if you want."

"No, that will be plenty, I have some things I need to take care of and I want to be on my way as soon as possible."

"Mr. Ray, that's all you ever do. Run to one place, than another."

"I know it seems that way, but I have important things to take care of today."

"Is it about the thing we find in Mrs. Ray's room?"

I keep my thoughts to myself about showing the folder to the police. Just how far would Jim go to get that folder? Was it possible he got so angry that he would confront Viv and kill her trying to get the information from her? And if so, how did he do it? Maybe I should run it by the professionals and see what they think.

I eat three bites of breakfast, I have no appetite. But Maria worries if I don't eat.

I grab the folder out of the locked drawer and notice the baggie I put in there with the strange substance. It couldn't hurt to bring this along and see if the police will analyze it. I can't shake the feeling the unknown substance may tie in with the death of Viv, or that I watch too many crime shows?"

I wait in the lobby of the Homicide Division with the folder tucked under my arm. My leg is twitching and the burning in my stomach has returned. I see Det. Andrews coming down the hallway talking to what I assume is a fellow detective. I get up quickly from my chair to intercept Det. Andrews.

"Mr. Raymonds. What are you doing here today? It's my day off."

"I have something you and Det. White should see. I shouldn't put it that way. No one should ever see what's in this folder."

I put the folder on his desk. "After you look through the photos, I will tell you how I think they tie in with Viv's murder. And it is murder, no doubt.

Let me remind you Mr. Raymonds. Did we not advise you to let us handle it?"

"Yes, but I didn't go looking for this evidence. Well, I did, but it's not what you might think."

He opens the folder and instantly appalled. "Jesus, you could have warned me!" He closes the folder, throws it on his desk and pushes his chair back. He is speechless and by the look on his face, the photos affected him just as they did me.

"My God, this stuff is hard to look at. Who is this guy? Is he on your so-called suspect list?"

"His name is James Marshall, but he goes by Big Jim. He was my wife's boss and ex client of mine."

"Your wife had these in her possession? Could Mrs. Raymonds be black mailing Mr. Marshall?"

"You- you got it all wrong detective. He showed up at the hospital after my...episode. We hadn't seen or heard from him in over a year."

"You might not have, but do we know that Mrs. Raymonds hadn't?"

"She hated that man! She wanted nothing to do with him. She forbid him from coming to our wedding. There is no way she would have kept in touch with him. Even to black mail him. He gives me some bullshit story that he came to offer his condolence. The real reason he was here was some important folder that was missing and he thought Viv might have it. He wanted me to look for it and as you can see I found it."

"Did Mr. Marshall tell you what was in the folder?"

"No. But I think he thought he could buy my silence."

"So, you are telling me the guy raping the young boy in these photos is Jim Marshall?"

"Yes, aka Big Jim. Now you see why I think he had a tremendous motive for murder."

"I agree that this Big Jim Marshall is a solid lead to work with. We will put him under surveillance and do a background check, see if he had any priors. With this evidence you brought us, he will be seeing the inside of a prison very soon. And that goes with or without him involved in your wife's death.

"In her murder! I will never be able to scrub those pictures away. I can't believe Viv never told me about them. Why? - Why would she keep that kind of secret to herself?

Det. Andrews shakes his head. "One thing I've learned working as a Detective. Sometimes there is no good answer for why people do what they do."

"Before I forget, I found something unusual at my house. It might be important, it might not. I reach in my coat pocket and set down the Ziploc baggie on his desk. He holds it up and looks at it through the ceiling lights. "I found it outside on the patio, leading into the room Viv died in."

"If this unknown substance was found where you say it was. I'm sure the Forensic Team took a sample."

"But what if they didn't?" I was not letting go of the idea that this substance had something to do with Viv's murder. I had a gut feeling, I can't shake."

"If it will let me get out of here and spend what little time of my day off I have left, than I will drop it off at the lab myself. Ok, Mr. Raymonds?"

"You can call my Bob, Det. Andrews."

I appreciate that Bob. And you can call me Detective Andrews." He smiles. He stands and shakes my hand. I know in an effort to move me along.

I had turned my cell phone to vibrate when I walked into Homicide Department. When I go to turn the ringer back on, I see I have three messages. I play them back and listen.

"HI-This is Buddy's Family Fish Farm. We would like to schedule a time to come out and do routine maintenance on your aquarium. We have not been able to reach the primary number on the account. Please give us a call at 555-3474. That's 555-FISH. Thank you."

I have to smile a bit. I always assumed Viv took care of our aquarium on her own. I wait for message 2.

Hello, Bob. This is Dr. Radcliff. I would really like to speak with you in person. I am back in town and can see you at your earliest convenience. Please call me at my office or my exchange. Thank you."

The voicemail states message number 3

"Mr. Ray this is Maria. Dr Radcliff called and say it is very important he speak with you. He say call him back at his office. I tell him to try your cell phone. Gracias."

I can't imagine what the urgency is? Then I remember the frantic message I left on his voicemail. He is probably checking to make sure I haven't done anything stupid. I dial his number on my cell expecting to get a voicemail, only after one ring I hear the deep baritone voice of the doctor. "This is Dr. Radcliff."

"Hey Doc. It's good to hear your voice. Look I'm sorry about the message I left you. I was in a dark place. I found something and let my imagination run wild."

"Glad to hear that you are doing better. I would really like to see you in person." Doc seems persistent.

"Doctor, really I'm ok. I don't need a therapy session."

"Bob, I'm in the office right now. Why don't you just swing by? I think you will find it very beneficial or for sure very intriguing."

When I arrive Dr. Radcliff's office door is locked, so I knock loudly. He opens the door he is not wearing his trademark sweat but what could only be described as a velour running outfit in a dark plumb color. "Sorry for the casual look. I'm not due back in the office for a few more days. Please come in."

His office is quiet, more so than usual. The blinds are closed, no faithful secretary Joan, no one waiting in the lobby and no soft music playing over the speaker.

"Doc, I told you I'm fine. In fact, I have some good news or maybe good news isn't the right word. Thanks to me, I think the cops will be making an arrest for Viv's murder soon."

"So, the case has been ruled a homicide? You never believed it was a suicide, did you?" He motions for us to sit on the couch in the lobby, not in his private office.

"I didn't. But then I got a whopper of a story from my business partner Jim Haverty about Vivian saying it would be better if she wasn't here."

"And you had never heard Mrs. Raymonds say anything like that before?"

"No. not me. She could get a little melancholy, but that doesn't matter. I'm pretty sure her ex-boss Big Jim Marshall is the one that killed my Viv."

Radcliff looks like he is trying to find a tactful way to ask me something. "And the police agree with you? They have evidence?"

"Not yet. But I gave them some disturbing photos of pedophile Marshall that Viv had. So there's the motive and I'm sure they will figure all the rest out. I gave them a sample of something that could turn out to be evidence and they will have him under surveillance soon."

"I see." Dr. Radcliff stands up and retrieves his briefcase and takes out a large book. He opens to a page he had marked with a yellow sticky note.

"Why did you want to meet Doc?" He shows what is written on the sticky note, Primarily Obsessional OCD. "I don't get it? You think I have this?"

"No I think Vivian's killer did. What I'm going to tell you will sound far fetch. But I want you to just listen. People with Primarily Obsessional OCD have frequent unwanted thoughts about harming themselves or other people. These thoughts can be quite violent and totally uncharacteristic to one's nature. Some common intrusive thoughts that overcome patients can be health, sexual orientation, even religion. Another aspect is responsibility. Let me read to you about this aspect. "An excessive concern over someone's well-being specifically believing by guilt; they have on purpose or inadvertently allowed someone to be hurt. People with this form have distressing and unwanted thoughts that can likely turn aggressive in nature."

"I got to say Doc, I am thoroughly confused. But let's cut to the chase. You have a name in mind."

"In fact, I do, but I don't think you will agree my suspect. It is your housekeeper Maria Sanchez."

"Give me a break! I listened to your lead up and I'm waiting for the big reveal and this is who you come up with? My little housekeeper? I don't know if you got too much sun, or not enough sleep or a blow to the head? This is ridiculous!" I feel my face turning red and the anger seeping in. I want to lash out at this absurd conclusion.

Dr. Radcliff can see it and sits next to me on the couch. He looks me directly in the eyes. "Bob let's look at it with an open mind, How did she react about when Viv brought different men over?"

"She felt sorry for me, I guess?"

"Would you say she felt guilty that she couldn't take away your pain? I think she saw the deep despair you were in and that turned her compulsive thoughts into a form of rage. You told me at several sessions you wished Vivian dead. Did you ever make that feeling known to Maria?"

"I don't know! But it doesn't matter. The killer is James Marshall, not Maria! She couldn't hurt Viv. I know it!"

"Even after she say how Vivian humiliated you? She lived with you and Vivian. Did she not hear the fights?

"So, you're saying Maria was what? In love with me? Jealous of Viv?" I stand up ready to leave.

"Robert, please come sit." I sit back down this time in a chair on the other side of the room, as far as way as possible from him. "I think Maria sees you has an honorable man and she loves that about you, a familiar love. And I think, if she is suffering from what I theorize, than in her mind it was her responsibility to take care of you. She would feel compelled to, just like a patient with OCD will feel compelled to wash their hands a 100 times a day. She would fixate on trying to solve the cause of her or her loved one distress. To be your protector."

"I feel queasy." I put my head down between my legs and try to breath. "And she thought murdering Vivian would protect me?!"

"Yes. In her mind, a sick mind. Maria thought she was bringing you peace. Now of course this is all conjecture. I am telling you to look at your housekeeper as a suspect in your wife's murder. She had opportunity, she had a motive in my assumption; the only thing I cannot speak to is means. I do not know how she committed the crime, only why."

"This seems insane, for lack of a better word. I agree Maria would do just about anything for me, but murder?!"

"I have an idea that might bring everything to light, if you can bring the investigating detectives on board. The only way this will works, is if detective's are in it a hundred percent."

On my drive home I tell myself to act as normal as possible. I don't want to extend any outward sign that something is up. When I pull in to the driveway I see Maria is out front picking up the mail from the box. She sees me and smiles and waves. She is such a friendly and hard-working woman, her loyalty was unquestioned. I don't have a chance to undo my seatbelt before she is at the car door trying to open it for me.

"Oh Mr. Ray, I am so glad you are home, I want to make you your favorite dinner."

"I never knew I had a favorite dinner, but I guess if anyone would know, it would be you."

"Please Mr. Ray. I have been with you a long time, I pay attention what you say after your dinner. You say many times, this is one of my favorite dinners."

"You got me, what is it that I like so much?"

"My chicken fried steak and mashed potatoes and gravy. You remember now?"

"My gosh you're absolutely correct! I love that meal. Shows me you know me better than I know myself."

"You please come in and I will fix you your drink and you just relax, read your mail, and I will bring you your dinner at your desk, is that fine for you?"

"Gee that sounds great, but I think I will take my dinner upstairs and no drink for me tonight. There are some files that need to be updated and then I'm going to catch up on my DVR."

I feel the best way not to crack under the pressure and say something suspicious is to keep my distance from her. Other than seeing her when she brings in my dinner, I avoid her all night. I have to admit she was right, that indeed was one of my favorite dinners. I watch television for a couple of hours, not really paying attention to any of my shows. All I could do is obsess on Radcliff's whole OCD theory. I would go along with this stupid plan to prove Maria's innocence. But it all hinged on the Wonder Twin agreeing to do it, and I didn't think they would appreciate my amateur meddling again.

I feel my eyelids get heavy. I don't bother hitting the remote to turn the TV off. I hope that the sounds from it will trick my sub conscience into avoiding a night of tossing and turning from anticipation and anxiety.

My worries were unwarranted because morning arrives with the curtain pulling ritual. "Good morning Mr. Ray, are you awake? She flutters around the room picking up the papers I pretended to update and my dinner dishes. She tries again a bit louder. "Mr. Ray would you like your breakfast in your bedroom today?"

"Good morning Maria. No breakfast for me today. I have another appointment today, so just some coffee please. I'll be down in a bit."

"Si, Mr. Ray. Are you sure nothing quick to eat?"

"No, but speaking of eats. You were right, that is my favorite dinner.

"Oh thank you, I knew for sure you like very much. The coffee is ready when you are.

I shower and dress with coffee in hand in 15 minutes. The mission today is to go to the detective and tell them Radcliff's plan and hope they agree to be involved in this absurd ruse to get Maria to confess to a crime I don't think she committed

As soon as I was out of eyesight, I pull over and call Det. Andrews, "Detective Andrews speaking."

"I'm glad you're in. I'm on my way in to talk with you and your sidekick."

"I'm sorry who is this?"

"Oh Jesus Christ! This is Bob Raymonds. Please tell me you have arrested James Marshall."

"James Marshall has been apprehended trying to flee the country. Cyber is going over his computer now."

I breathe a sigh of relief. "So, he did it? He killed Viv?"

"I'm sorry Bob, we haven't found any evidence linking him to your wife's death. He is being charged with rape of a minor and child pornography and a slew of other crimes, but not the murder of Vivian Raymonds."

"I will be there in 20 minutes I need to talk to you and Det. White."

"That will work, Detective White is on his way into the office."

I storm into the Homicide Division and there's moment of silence from the activity going on in the room. Once everyone sees I'm not a crazed gunman they return to whatever they are doing without missing a beat. I see Detective White pushing the door open while holding a cup of coffee, "I heard you were on your way with some vital information. Let me guess, it was Colonel Mustard with the candlestick?" He snickers, "I can't wait to hear what you got."

Det. White sits at his desk, removes the lid off his Styrofoam cup and sips his coffee. He doesn't like the taste so he adds two packets of sugar. Det. Andrews very politely pulls out a chair for me near his desk. "Here, have a seat, would you like a coffee?"

"No, thank you. My stomach couldn't handle it any way."

"Well, like I told you on the phone. James Marshall has been arrested but this department nor have two other agencies found any evidence linking him to your wife's murder. I pretty sure once you didn't hand over the folder, he must have suspected you went to the police."

"That sicko knew is goose was cooked." Det. White says.

"So where does that leave us?" I ask.

Det. White doesn't like my question. "Mr. Raymonds there is no us! We are still working this case, that hasn't changed. But let me guess. You have another suspect added to your murder board?"

"I might." I'm reluctant to mention Dr. Radcliff's wild theory.

"Before we hear what you have to say Mr. Dick Tracy. Would you like to know what that substance is you brought us?"

"I would. That's why I brought it in." I suddenly worry that the unknown substance would now be damaging to Maria.

"The lab says the substance consisted of powdered calcium carbonate and linseed oil, and other words its window putty."

Window putty, so it wasn't some deadly agent like Anthrax. That was good news, yet I still have a nagging feeling.

Det. White asks. "Ok let's hear your latest info that is going to crack this case wide open? Give us the name of the person or persons that moved to the top of your list. Because it wasn't Randy Lockford and it looks like James Marshall didn't do it, so who you got now?"

To remain calm I take a deep breath in and begin. "For me to prove if this person is guilty or not I will need your help."

"What kind of help?" Det. Andrews asks.

"An elaborate charade of sorts."

I start with Dr. Radcliff's diagnosis and his suspicion. I rattle on and I soon notice the deafening silence in the room; I pause and look at them. They don't have their mouths open with a distant stare, but I can tell I piqued their interest.

"Before I go any further, do you guys have any feedback? Do you think it's worth a try?"

Detective Andrews is the first to speak. "Police can use deception on suspects in a variety of ways. She can't just confess. We have innocent people do that. We would need to know how she did it. What do you think Ryan?"

"I think it's a far reach, partner. But if you're sold on it, and she can put the pieces together, I'm in. Let's get this ruse started. I say there's no time like the present."

"She should be home all day. My plan is I'll go home and you show up in say, two hours. I'll be stressed out enough so she notices. I'll pace around worried saying that you are both on your way and by the time you get here she'll be in full protective mode, I think. I don't know how it all works with this so called primary OCD. Or if she even has this thing."

"Maybe she was hoping she'd be in your will and then she would off you." Det. White scoffs

"Oh my God Detective! Please just try this." Det. Andrews nods a yes motion.

Det. White wisecracks. "We know what we are doing. Don't screw up your end." And with that I head home to play my part.

I pull in the driveway and park in my usual spot. I walk right in, I can hear the vacuum going upstairs, but don't call out Maria's name to let her know I'm home. I head to the Rec. Room and start making a lot of noise. I sit in my chair, head in my hands and wait. Voila, the door opens and Maria walks in.

"Mr. Ray, is everything okay? You look like you upset."

"I don't know Maria? The police called me a few minutes ago and told me they want to talk with me. I asked about what. All they told me to be home and not to leave. I've been around law enforcement long enough to know they may be ready to make an arrest."

"Oh no, how can that be? I think they are trying to scare you. They can't do that Mr. Ray, they don't have no proof." She begins to rub her hands raw with the towel tucked in her apron.

"Well I really don't know why they are coming over but it does not look good for me."

"Oh, how I hate to see you worry like this, can I fix you something to eat, maybe you feel better with some food. You had no breakfast, you need to eat something."

"Maria, you are always at my side, but some things just can't be fixed with food or loyalty. I'm not hungry. I'm going upstairs, please come and get me when the detectives arrive."

"Si Mr. Ray, I will let you know."

I head up to my room feeling the bait has been taken. Now wait and see if the detectives could pull off their part. I could not help but hope Dr. Radcliff was a 100% wrong, the thought of seeing Maria taken off in handcuffs almost brings me to tears.

Time seems to drag, I'm anxious and don't know what to do with myself. I turn on the television but can't concentrate. I try reading, but keep reading the same line over and over. I give up on anything to entertain myself and just sit on the end of the bed and think back to when Viv and I moved in and we interviewed for a live-in housekeeper. We interviewed dozens of applicants but it was an easy choice once Maria had her turn in the interview process. Looking back that seems like a lifetime ago and by God it was.

I hear tapping on the door and the low tones of Maria saying, "Mr. Ray, the police are here." From the sound of her voice, I can tell she has been crying.

"Please tell them I will be down in just a minute."

"Si. Mr. Ray."

I go in the bathroom look at myself in the mirror. I'm about to throw some water on my face and comb my hair back, but the disheveled look would have more impact on Maria. I question if I'm doing the right thing. I look at the gold wedding band on my left hand. No matter what, Viv didn't deserve to die.

I head down the stairs for what could be the end of this horrible ordeal. Each step I take down the stairs makes my heart beat faster. I hit the landing and head directly to the recreation room knowing that's where Maria would bring them. I walk in and see the two detectives looking at my beautiful aquarium.

"It's a beautiful set up Mr. Raymonds." Det. Andrews says.

"Yeah, I bet it cost you a chunk of change?"

"Yep it did, but I found it well worth the money, I find it very serene and enjoy the peacefulness of it all. But you guys didn't come to talk about fish."

"No, you're right, Mr. Raymonds. We are here on official business, we have a warrant for your arrest."

Maria shouts- "NO! This can't be. You are wrong." She wags her index finger in their direction. "Mr. Ray would never hurt Mrs. Raymonds. I've been here long time. I never see Mr. Ray even touch her, no matter how mean she was to him."

"Don't waste your breath Maria. The detectives have always thought I was the one that killer her. I want you to let all phone calls go to the recorder, don't answer the door. I will call Mr. Haverty. I am sure I will be out on bail and be back home in no time/"

"You better not put the cart before the horse Mr. Raymonds, as you well know, it will be up to the judge to decide if a bail will be set. Now, put your hands behind your back." Det. Andrews says.

"Detectives do you really think cuffs are necessary? I'm come willingly

"It is protocol in our department." Det. White spins me around and handcuffs me. He seems to be enjoying his roll.

"No! No! "Maria shouts in a panic voice as she tries to stop the handcuffing process."

"Please stand back ma'am." The instructions are given in a no-nonsense tone. "Mr. Raymonds will be coming with us. Please do as you're told."

She makes the sign of the cross on herself and stands back as told. I'm lead out the door towards an unmarked police car, Det. Andrews gives me a quizzical look as our backs our turned from her view. Det. White says in a low voice, "it looks like your wrong- again."

"Is she still watching?"

"Yes." Det. Andrews whispers.

"Go ahead, put me in the back of the car and make it a little rough."

Det. White opens the squad door and forcibly pushes my head down as he puts me in the back-seat. I yelp out in pain, "Please, I have a bad back."

I hear Maria sob, "Querido Dios! Mr, Ray"

Det. Andrews goes around to get to the driver's seat and looks back at me. "It looks like your housekeeper is holding her ground."

I have nothing to say, I slowly shake the 'no' motion with my head down. As Det. White is climbing in the passenger seat of the car, Det. Andrews motions his head and eyes toward the front door. "Look who's headed our direction."

I look up and let out an audible sigh. "God! I had hoped Dr. Radcliff was wrong."

Maria comes right up to the car and Det. Andrews steps out. "Ma'am, I'm going to ask you to step back inside the house please. There is nothing you can do for him right now."

With a soft voice but clearly loud enough to be heard. "Please come back in. I want to prove to you Mr. Ray did not kill his wife. I know this... because I did."

Det. White steps out of the car and stands with his arms resting on the open door. "If this is some ploy to keep Mr. Raymonds out of jail, I will not appreciate it. I'll charge you with hindering an arrest and filing a false report, do I make myself clear?"

"Si, yes. I understand very much. You come back in and I tell you everything." Det. Andrews helps me out of the back of the squad car, he doesn't uncuff me. We head back into the house. Maria is two steps ahead of us, she reaches the door first, and she pushes it open to its widest position and stands back for us to enter. The whole procession from the car to the door was done in stone cold silence.

Maria is the first to speak. She wrings her hands on her trusted towel. "I tell you what I do. You will see Mr. Ray had nothing to do with any of this."

Det. Andrews does his diligence, "You have the right to remain silent. Anything you say can and will be used against you in a court of law. You have the right to speak to an attorney and to have an attorney present during questioning. If you cannot afford any attorney one will be provided for you. Do you understand the rights I have read to you? Would you like me to read them in Spanish?"

"No, I understand."

"It started day before I kill Mrs. Raymonds. I go outside and bring the little torch."

"Wait." Det. Andrews says. "What do you mean little torch?"

"I don't know what you call it, my husband always called it a torch. Here let me go and get it and I show you."

"Det. White will accompany you."

They come back and Det. White is holding a small cylinder propane torch.

"Years ago, when I worked with my husband he showed me how to fix broken windows. You heat the putty so you could peel it away. That is what I did. I remove glass from the patio door so I can reach-in and undo bolt lock.

I had already taken some cardboard and made a funnel with point on end. I fill it with water and put in freezer, when it froze I slide it out and use that."

"Use it how Mrs. Sanchez?"

"I stab Mrs. Raymonds."

"Oh Maria, why?" I blurt out.

Det. White tells me, "Mr. Raymonds, please refrain from saying anything."

"I use gloves so not leave any of my marks on the window and because the ice was slippery and cold to hold."

"You mean the latex- vinyl gloves the kind doctor's use?" Det. Andrews asks.

"Yes, it's the kind I use when I do the bathrooms and sinks. I unbutton her blouse and lift up her bra so ice knife goes into her heart much easier, then fix her clothes back and throw ice knife in fish tank.""

Det. White, "Didn't she fight you?"

"Oh no. I bring her drink like she has every day when she read her mail only this time I put her relaxing pills in drink. She has taken for many years. She says they calm her calm her down. I don't use a lot, so police won't think anything is wrong. I have enough time to do my job and put everything back as it was before. I burn gloves, window was easy to put back. I know I leave little bits of the old putty and try and find them but I didn't find them all."

When she says that- the detectives look at each other, then they look in my direction,

"Maria, may I call you Maria? Asks Det. Andrews.

"Yes. I don't like being called Mrs. Sanchez. I have been separated from him for years so I like being called Maria much better."

"Then Maria could you tell me and my partner what drove you to the point of planning and committing this murder?"

"I used to like Mrs. Raymonds. She was a nice lady but Mr. Ray started working real hard and came home late. Sometimes he work so hard, he's too tired to drive home he stay at office. Even when he come home he would work. Read and make calls. It got much worse when he got big baseball player job, he work all the time.

She looks at me, "you remember Mr. Ray?" I just nod.

"That made them argue. She get so mad at him. She would yell that he cared more about his stupid job than her."

"Maria, do you remember if it got physical?"

"As the baseball player case went on the more upset she got. I remember one night I hear a crash and think someone fell on some furniture but when I get in room I see Ms. Viv throwing things at Mr. Ray. When I go in room, she runs out and she say she wishes Mr. Ray was dead. I see things are getting worse every day but I never think she would start bringing in men to the house when Mr. Ray at work It hurt me but I had to tell him what was going on. He needed to get her out of our lives."

My mind is racing. I destroyed the two most important women in my life. How could I be so blind?

"When you told Mr. Raymonds what did he say or do?"

"He say it was best that they stayed in different bedrooms. He also say he would talk to her. I think- no more talk. She should go. Mr. Ray told her no more men in the house, go to a motel. But she no listen, she had men in the house. She would even go out of her way to embarrass Mr. Ray. But he never let her know how mad and sad he was. He would just walk away. I think that made her madder. I feel so sorry for him, I want to end this good man's suffering. Please may I get a drink of water?"

"Det. White will get you one. Why don't you continue?"

"You know what I did, how I did it. What more is there to say? Let Mr. Ray go."

Det. White returns with a glass of water and hands it to Maria. She slowly drinks, as if this will be the last water she will ever have. She sets the half full glass on a table and folds her towel neatly on her lap.

"There is one more thing. I use one of Mr. Ray's coats that night. I didn't want to leave, how you say?" She searches for the word... skin on the window frame. My gloves were not long enough so I use one of Mr. Ray's coat when I reach up to unlock. I thought it was coat Mr. Ray didn't wear."

She looks directly at me, tears are forming in her eyes. "Mr. Ray I never notice the spot until you ask me to take to cleaners. I worry so much that the police find the stain on your coat and blame you. I truly am sorry. I just wanted to protect you. I so sorry."

Tears flow now. She picks up the folded towel on her lap and wipes her eyes." I'm glad this is all over. I worry sick every day and night they come for you and you did nothing bad. Now I don't worry no more."

The detectives stand up in unison. Det. White tells me to stand and turn around, he removes my handcuffs. As I turn back around I see the opposite process taking place with my loyal Maria. I can feel the tears now streaming down my face.

"Please Mr. Ray don't be sad I will be fine. I just want you to be happy again like you used to be."

"Maria, I will call one of the best lawyers I know, my partner Mr. Haverty. We have been known to pull off some miracles in the courtroom. I don't think your case will need any divine intervention."

She smiles at me as she was being led out of the house.

"So you are going to help the person that murder your wife?' Det. White asks.

"You heard her detective. Dr. Radcliff was right. He diagnosed her with that obessional disease. She needs psychiatric help, not prison."

I can't watch her being put in the squad car, my heart is breaking for someone who literally would give up their life for me.

I go to the phone and call the office. I get the standard greeting, "Raymonds and Haggerty Law Offices."

"Hello, Michelle it's Bob. Is Jim in?"

"Yes, let me put you through."

"Jim Haverty speaking."

"Jim, I need your help."

"Anything Bob, you know that."

"How do you feel about taking on a murder case? The police just took Maria from the house in handcuffs."

"What are you talking about?"

"Maria Sanchez just confessed to killing Viv. She's gonna need your services, that is, if you're up to it?"

"I will do whatever you need me to do. Are you okay?"

"I can't be her defense lawyer. I'm too close to her."

"Slow down there buddy. How do you know she really committed this crime and isn't confessing to keep the police from framing you?"

"She just told us on how she committed this crime. She took us step by step through the whole process. She did it Jim!"

"I believe you and I'd be more than willing to defend her. Of course I will discount my rate." I know he is trying to lighten my mood. I'm just not ready to laugh.

"I can't thank you enough for being there when I need you most."

"You know Bob, it will be good working side-by-side with you again. Just like old times."

"Jim, I don't know if it will ever be like old times again."

THE END

Printed in the United States
By Bookmasters